KILL OR CURE

KILL OR CURE

A DYSTOPIAN YOUNG ADULT NOVEL

PIXIE BRITTON

Matador
9 Priory Business Park,
Wistow Road, Kibworth Beauchamp,
Leicestershire, LE8 0RX
Tel: 0116 279 2299
Email: books@troubador.co.uk
Web: www.troubador.co.uk/matador
Twitter: @matadorbooks

ISBN 978 1788038 485

British Library Cataloguing in Publication Data.
A catalogue record for this book is available from the British Library.

Printed and bound in the UK by 4edge limited
Typeset in 11pt Adobe Garamond Pro by Troubador Publishing Ltd, Leicester, UK

Matador is an imprint of Troubador Publishing Ltd

For Adam

LAST RESORTS

As I stand barefoot in the forest, the sun is coming up over the horizon. This is my favourite time of day; the moist cool air prickles against my skin, and I feel the damp moss between my toes. I close my eyes and focus on the wind blowing lazily through the trees. The birds start to sing their morning songs, unaware of the dangers lurking in the depths of the forest. I take a deep breath and hold it, savouring the fresh forest smell, letting it fill my lungs and not wanting to let it go. This is my true home; this is where I feel at peace. I breathe out, smile and relax. I could stay in this moment forever.

In the distance, interrupting the orchestra of nature echoing through the forest, is the unmistakable shuffling of feet. Instantly alert, my eyes spring open and I feel as though I have been shaken from a dream. I strain to hear above the deafening sound of blood pumping in my ears, as I frantically search for them hiding in the tree line. Flanked at my side is my best friend Will, standing there poised and deadly, staring at me with his unblinking green eyes. He gently nods at me and confirms that he heard it too. A boyish smile creeps across his face as he slowly draws his sword from its sheath; this is one of Will's favourite pastimes.

I stand there frozen, as that familiar sinking feeling gnaws in the pit of my stomach: the anticipation of what lies ahead. Will points in the direction of the sound, and my fears are quickly confirmed by the resonant moaning of the Dead. Without hesitating, he runs fearlessly towards them. I start running and desperately try to keep up as my long hair stings my bare shoulders. I quicken my pace and lengthen my stride, being careful not to trip on tree roots. I'm glad that we are barefoot; hopefully they haven't heard us coming.

The birds have stopped singing, and for a moment the forest is deathly silent. The putrid smell of rotting flesh consumes the both of us, even before we can see them clearly. My eyes begin to water, as the usual wave of nausea rolls over me. Even after all this time, I clutch my mouth to stop myself from retching. Swallowing hard, I focus all my senses on the five Infected dragging their rancid bodies through the thick density of the trees. Out of the corner of my eye, Will holds up three fingers, silently confirming that he will take the three Infected on his right. Holding myself centred, I give Will a curt nod, confirming that I know the plan.

In unison, we silently circle our prey on opposite sides, taking cover behind the trees and never taking our eyes off the Dead. Swords are raised, muscles tensed; they are only a few metres away now. My pulse quickens, and then in one heart-sinking moment, an Infected spots me. A moan gurgles deep inside its chest as it slowly staggers towards me. With outstretched arms and snarling face, it reaches for me hungrily and closes the distance between us.

Clutching my sword tightly, I grit my teeth and in one

swift motion, I slice through its neck, decapitating it. Its head thuds on the forest floor, flicking black congealed blood in every direction. The wretched thing is still chomping, rabid for human flesh. I spin around, confronted by the other Infected and shove it with the hilt of my sword. It crashes to the ground, with arms and legs flailing. Before it can climb to its feet, I mercilessly slam the end of my sword down, ending its dismal existence.

To my right Will is standing triumphantly among the bodies, covered in gore and rotten flesh. He walks up to the decapitated head, finishes it off and swiftly chucks away his spoiled jacket. I look away, feeling shameful with the familiar guilt rising; they were once human like us. Will, knowing what I was thinking, says, "Its better off this way, Alyx."

He reaches out to me and reassuringly places his hand on my shoulder, staring at me with concerned eyes. I know he's right of course – they are no longer human; they are monsters trapped in a human shell – but it still doesn't make it easy. Will has always maintained that if he was ever turned, he would rely on me to end the suffering and assures me that he would do the same.

In this messed-up world that we live in, most folks have similar pacts with their loved ones, which is the bleak reality that we have to survive in. To that end, we must tell ourselves that someone somewhere is thankful that we have ended the eternal pain of their loved ones today, that they can now rest in peace and the never-ending hunger for human flesh is finally over. I hope with all my heart and soul that I never have to carry through with this promise, for as long as we both live. I try to swallow, but my mouth has become as dry as sandpaper.

"Let's get the yarrow and get out of here. When Joe realises that I'm gone, he's gonna go nuts!"

Will looks at me steadily. His face shines with sweat in the morning sun as he tenses his angular jaw. Using the back of his hand, he wipes away the grime from his forehead and pushes his sandy hair out of his eyes. With a solemn expression, he gently nods his head, a reminder of why we were here in the first place.

My twelve-year-old brother, Tommy, became sick five days ago with some kind of flu virus. Some folks in town are panicking that it's the infection, the one that brings you back to life and makes you want to eat your own family, but they are wrong, way wrong. They have to be, and that's the end of it. I know it looks similar–the high fever and the sickness–but it could be anything, and when he gets better, they will all be pretty embarrassed for not having any faith.

Feeling a little shaky, I quickly scout around the forest floor and tuck my hair behind my ears, searching for this 'magical' yarrow flower. I heard that it's supposed to reduce fever, and right now I'm willing to try anything. Will points to a bunch of tiny white flowers at the base of a tree and starts pulling at its roots.

"How much do we need?" he asks.

I shrug my shoulders when I realise that I have no idea.

"Let's get as much as we can. Let's face it, when Joe finds out that I have been outside the walls… I'll be on lockdown."

In the distance, I hear the bone-chilling shriek of the Dead echoing through the forest. My eyes instantly meet Will's as he confirms, "That's fine, but let's do it quickly."

We scrabble around on our hands and knees, stuffing as much yarrow as we can find into our pockets. I hope this stuff is as good as they say it is. If it doesn't work, I don't know what we are going to do. I grind my teeth with frustration at the thought of failure and angrily rip the tiny flowers from their roots.

As I dig my fingers into the dirt, ramming mud and stones painfully under my nails, my inner voice prattles with irritation at the injustice of Tommy's sickness. The never-ending chorus of "why us?" reverberates in my head, making me want to scream. In this new world, I bet millions of others have asked the exact same question at some point in their too-short lives.

As I become more and more consumed in my own angry thoughts, another moan resonates through the trees, but much closer this time. We are pushing our luck now. A small group we can handle, but a horde of Infected is a different story. That's the difference between surviving and being torn to pieces by the mouths of the dead.

Knowing that we are running out of time, Will stops me in my tracks. With glazed eyes I exhale loudly, swallowing back the quivering lump that's threatening to rise in my throat. Without making eye contact with Will, I stiffly climb from my knees and start to jog back to the town wall in silence.

As I find my stride, I focus on the cool morning air blowing against my skin to dispel the images of my sick little brother. But the more I try, the more I see them. Images of his rosy, youthful appearance replaced with a grey ghost of his former self. Images of his now skeletal frame with eyes that are red, raw and swollen.

I stifle a sob from my chest, not wanting to appear vulnerable in front of Will. I must stay strong and keep it together, for myself and for Tommy. I have to remind myself he can't be infected because he hasn't been bitten. Hell, he hasn't even been outside the walls, which is the only way he could have been bitten. It's just some weird flu virus, and in a few days he'll be back to normal, driving me nuts again. He has to get better and that's the end of it.

We quickly reach the town wall and survey the area for any soldiers in the surrounding watch towers. The town's defence is stationed at five posts at the edge of the compound. If one of the guards spots us out here unauthorised we would be in serious trouble. As I take cover, the soldiers appear to be occupied by something. I smirk when I realise they're actually tucking in to their breakfasts. Another day of sloppy porridge out of old cans.

Will quickly seizes the opportunity and automatically goes down on one knee, interlinks his hands and offers me a leg up. Unlike Will, who could give a Viking a run for his money, I'm vertically challenged, even for a girl. He looks up at me and grins mischievously, clearly waiting for his moment to tease me.

Before he can open his mouth, I take pleasure in slapping my dirty foot in his hand and then deliberately flick some mud directly into his face. His smile drops momentarily as he gives me a withering look. Catching me off guard, he suddenly launches me into the air. I grab the edge of the wall with my fingertips and slowly struggle to pull myself up, being careful not to graze my elbows against the solid stones.

At the top, I turn to face Will and sit on the edge of the towering wall feeling drained; I haven't slept much since Tommy became sick. Noting my expression, he doesn't waste any time. Will walks a few paces away from the wall, eyeing it steadily. Narrowing his focus, he runs hard and explosively leaps for the top edge. With muscles straining, he only just grabs it and manages to pull himself up after a few grunts and some cursing. Trying to lighten the mood, he digs me in the ribs.

"Thanks for the assistance. Your enthusiasm was overwhelming."

Feeling completely distracted, I can't find the words to retort. I open my mouth to give him my usual quippy response, but I frankly don't have the energy. Studying my face, he exhales loudly and puts his arms around my shoulders.

"I know Tommy's unwell right now, but he's going to get better. He's not infected, Ally."

I nod my head in agreement. "I know he's not, but I don't know what I would do without…"

My voice fades as the image of an infected Tommy flashes to the forefront of my mind again. Feeling agitated, I realise I need to get back home to my family. With that thought, I drop off the wall into the town compound and grab my boots, quickly followed by Will.

The wide streets are eerily quiet, but as the morning sun rises higher in the sky, the town will shortly burst into life. The hunters will leave the town compound in search of edible meat, and the harvesters will gather vegetables from the fields. Each and every one of us has an important role to play to keep our society safe from the Dead that haunt us.

Will's home is at the edge of town and is one of the original houses that existed in Merope, before the spread of the infection. His two-storey house is one of a few homes that is actually made from bricks. Most folks had to construct their houses from wood from the forest, so the homes tend to be single-storey cabins with a tiny plot of land out back. This mishmash of housing is a stark reminder of what life used to be like pre-infection; a life where monsters only existed in stories and when humans were at the top of the food chain.

Will starts to walk even slower, almost dragging his feet. I know that he is dreading the wrath of his mum. She can be pretty scary at times, and when she learns that he snuck out this morning, she will be mad for sure. With his house in view, he empties the yarrow he collected from his pockets and smiles at me lopsidedly.

"Wish me luck!"

Smirking at him as I start to walk away, I say "I think you're going to need a miracle... not luck!"

Will walks up the path and approaches the front door. Before he enters the threshold, I call out, "Thanks for coming with me today."

He smiles at me with his twinkling green eyes and then quickly disappears into his home.

As I start to walk down the dusty road, I swear I can faintly hear his mum shouting. Eager to get home myself, I stealthily make my way through the empty streets and approach the 'newer' part of Merope where cabins are crammed in closely together, leaving no room for growth or privacy; where no one can even fart without their neighbours knowing about it. Some of these so-called cabins were skilfully crafted and look like tiny homes, others look downright shabby with corrugated roofs that are barely secure and have serious potential of collapsing. Luckily ours isn't that bad. Joe is pretty handy when it comes to construction and resourceful during the raids.

I eventually arrive at the street where my own cabin is, and Joe is sitting in his usual spot on the porch, smoking a cigarette, evidently exhausted. Joe is my uncle and unofficially adopted us when we were kids after my folks died during the first spread of the infection. Even though he's my uncle, he looks like he could be my dad; Joe, Tommy and I all have the same signature light brown eyes that we all inherited from my grandpa, but where Tommy and Joe have my grandpa's square jaw, I have the same round face and button nose as my mum. Joe has no wife or his own kids. It's just the three of us left.

Over the years, Joe has sacrificed a lot for us. He used to be a soldier in the government's army, but after he discovered that the town we lived in had been overrun by Infected, he left the squad to look after us. After all this time, Joe still has a 'soldier' look about him. He always maintains his short brown hair, a habit from his army days. His face and arms are deeply tanned from sitting out on the front porch, and his eyes have wrinkles around them from too much sun. Even though he's only forty-one years old, his faraway eyes hide years of torment from his tour in the military, which makes him seem older than he actually is. I've asked him to tell me about the early days, when the infection first spread, but he refuses to speak of them.

Since we came here, he has sold weapons in the market that he's either crafted himself or found during the raids. We don't have much these days, but we have enough to survive. Since the spread of the infection, that's all anyone wants to do. As soon as he sees me coming, he stands up with a serious expression on his face.

"Please tell me, Ally, that you ain't been outside the damn walls this morning... have you, kid?"

He stares at me angrily; he knows that I have been outside the walls, so there's no point lying. I nod my head steadily and reach for the yarrow stuffed in my pockets. I hold out the tiny, wiry flowers and present them to him.

"Look, please don't be mad. I wanted to get some yarrow for Tommy to see if we can get the fever down. I'm sorry. I just can't stand here and do nothing."

His face flushes with anger. "So, you thought that putting your own life at risk was worth trying to get some herb that probably won't even do anything? Jeez, Alyx, you're seventeen years old! Too young to be out there by yourself taking on Infected."

I open my mouth to justify myself further but quickly realise that I'm better off keeping quiet. Joe exhales loudly before sitting back down on the top step and taking a deep drag on his cigarette.

"I know you're trying to help, kid, but there are other ways, okay! Don't make me tell you again."

He leans over and grabs a knife from the huge pile that needs to be sharpened, shoving the hilt straight into my hand.

"Make yourself useful by sharpening these up. I'll be inside with Tommy."

I stare at the pile, feeling deflated. I was hoping to spend some time with Tommy this morning. As Joe gets up to leave, he hesitates by the front door, wavering uncertainly. His shoulders slump forward as he exhales loudly.

"Give me the damn yarrow, and tell me what the hell I'm supposed to do with it."

I turn and look at his sad eyes; he's clearly as fraught as I am. He usually wouldn't even entertain the idea of using herbal medicine, but I guess it shows just how desperate he really is. Without saying anything, I walk past him into our makeshift kitchen at the back of our house to brew the flowers, hoping with all my heart that Joe is wrong.

THEY DON'T TEACH THIS AT SCHOOL

I finish sharpening the knives sometime around midday and stretch my legs out in front of me, momentarily basking in the spring sun. Knowing that I need to relieve Joe, I stand up to get the blood flowing back into my legs. I hate pins and needles. The yarrow seemed to work, but only temporarily. Joe said that Tommy even had a little colour back in his face, but after forty-five minutes, the colour quickly faded, and he started puking uncontrollably again. Before I can get inside, Joe joins me out on the porch.

"Can you look after Tommy for a while?"

I nod solemnly. "Why don't we try getting him in the bath? It will probably help the pain."

Joe shakes his head with dismay. "Every time I have tried getting him out of bed, he screams the house down. Figured he was better off where he was."

Feeling a little desperate, I say, "If I heat the water for the bath now, we can wait until he's passed out asleep and then just carry him in there. I'm sure he can't be comfortable as he is."

Joe has a thoughtful expression on his face as he rubs his brow, with weariness. He looks over his shoulder, calculating my offer.

"You get the fire cooking, and I'll go check on him."

I quickly go outside to the back of the house and grab a few logs from our store pile. While the fire begins to roar, I fill up five metal canisters of water from the tank and hang them over the burning embers to boil. Five canisters of water for a bath is considered a luxury; after all, water is rationed, as with everything in Merope. I can't even remember the last time I had a steaming hot bath; most folks have a lukewarm wash at best.

As soon as I see the little bubbles begin to dance and pop in the canisters, I grab Joe's iron-casting mitts and run the water inside. I dash in and out the house, being careful not to slop any precious water on the way. Joe opens the bedroom door and nods his head at me, confirming that Tommy must be sound asleep. I follow him into the dim, stagnant room that is Tommy's bedroom. The curtains are drawn, giving the room a gloomy, dank appearance. I nervously step over the threshold as the stale smell of vomit and sweat hits the back of my throat, making my eyes water.

In the corner of the room, Tommy is curled up asleep with his sheets tangled around him. Joe slowly approaches the bed and tentatively pulls back the covers, exposing a now tiny Tommy so wet with perspiration that his pyjamas are stuck to his skin, and his hair is glued to his face. I stifle a sob at the sight of him; he's even worse than yesterday. I notice that as he sleeps, his breaths are slow and laboured, a new worrying symptom that he's developed overnight. Joe looks to me for reassurance, but I stand there rooted to the spot, so appalled by Tommy's appearance that I am unable to do anything.

Not wasting any more time, Joe reaches beneath

Tommy and pushes his hands underneath his bony frame. He stirs uneasily, almost flinching from his touch. In one swift motion, Joe lifts him from his spoiled bed, holding him close to his body. Tommy's eyes fling open, as he lets out an ear-piercing shriek. His face distorts as he claws at Joe, desperate to be released. I quickly open the door, making way for Joe to go through to the bathroom.

He strides out, struggling to hold onto Tommy as he thrashes erratically in his arms. Tommy is fighting so much that Joe nearly drops him straight into the bath. As soon as his body hits the water, though, something strange happens; he stops thrashing his limbs and lies there in a catatonic state, staring at the ceiling. I stand there too stunned to move as Joe lunges forward and reflexively feels for a pulse in his neck.

Joe bows his head and exhales loudly. "He's still breathing."

I sigh with relief, completely shocked by what happened. For a heart-breaking moment, I thought Tommy had actually turned. Uncertain of how much more of this I could take, I sit on the floor and rest my back against the wall. Completely resigned, Joe joins me and kneels beside the bath, wets a sponge in the warm water and gently squeezes it over Tommy's hair.

I close my eyes and focus on my own breathing. "It's not flu, is it? What if he is infected and the virus has mutated? What if it's airborne?"

Joe looks to Tommy, who is completely unaware of our presence and continues to stare at the ceiling.

"Well, if it is airborne, then this is the beginning of the end for all of us."

With a bleak expression, Joe leans over the bath and momentarily studies Tommy's face. He begins to clean the dried sweat from his forehead and stares at him with tired eyes.

"You know, when I look at you both, I see so much of your mum. Sometimes it's almost like she's still here."

He pauses and grabs the edge of the bath hard enough to turn his knuckles white. In that moment of pure vulnerability, I remember that this can't be easy for Joe: looking after your sister's children, one of which is very sick. He was thrown into fatherhood without warning and has had little time to grieve the loss of his own family. In this new screwed-up world, I guess we are all orphans to the Dead in one way or another.

"I hope we're doing the right thing here, kid. I really do."

Lost in my own thoughts, I nod my head steadily and chew my bottom lip until it hurts. I miss my parents every day, so much so it makes me ache. They died trying to save us. The nightmares from that day still haunt me today. If it wasn't for their selflessness, Tommy and I would have died for sure. The ironic thing is we damn nearly died from starvation, hiding in that cupboard waiting to be rescued; I have never been so pleased to see Joe's face in my life.

Since they died, I have always tried to be a good role model for Tommy, but seeing him like this makes me feel as though I have failed as a sister, failed to protect him in the same way our parents protected us. As I fight back my own tears, Joe steadily slides Tommy's pyjama top over his head as he continues to lay there unmoving. He drops the soaked jersey on the floor and turns back to comfort

Tommy. He grabs the sponge, wiping it across Tommy's chest, cleaning him. I put my head in my hands, feeling dazed, still desperately trying to hold back the tears that are threatening to spill down my rosy cheeks.

Suddenly, Joe jumps up from his knees and shakes his head. In a blur, he spins around and pulls me to my feet and starts to drag me towards the bathroom door. Completely exacerbated, and with my breath caught in my throat, I choke out, "What the hell is going on?"

He stares at me, face white as a ghost and full of panic. "Tommy's infected!"

As soon as the words leave Joe's mouth, I feel as though I have been punched in the stomach. Blood drains from my face, making me feel as though I'm going to pass out. He pushes me into the threshold of the lounge and reaches for the gun in his belt. As he slams the door in my face, my worst nightmare has finally been realised: Tommy is going to turn.

I was only six years old the day that our village was overrun by the Infected. It had started like any other day. The sun was blaring, so all of the windows were wide open. My dad and I were sitting on the lounge floor with Tommy, who was rolling around on a colourful, soft rug that my mum had stitched by hand. My mum looked on as she stood in front of the stove, boiling water for tea. It's strange how an ordinary day can change in a flash.

We never saw them coming. They were in the house before we could even think about escaping. My dad grabbed Tommy, who was writhing and screaming with all the commotion, and shoved him into my arms. Dad yelled at me, his face crimson with rage, to hide in the wardrobe and to not come out under any circumstances. He pushed a heavy table across the doors to make sure of that. That was the last time that I saw him alive. I don't remember crying at the time, although I probably did. All I remember is the sound of white noise filling my ears as I pressed my tiny face against the gap in the wardrobe doors. I watched them fight until the end.

As I stand outside the bathroom door, struggling to breathe, the same deafening white noise screams in my ears. I grab my head as my legs buckle beneath me, slamming my knees into the floor. Before I know it, I am sobbing uncontrollably. Making myself into a tiny ball on the floor, my heart feels as though it has been ripped from my chest, leaving a gaping wound behind. Hot tears stream down my face as I beg for the pain to stop. He's only a kid. Why isn't this happening to me? It should be me.

The world around me begins to sway as dark spots creep into my vision. How will I live without him? I'm not sure I can. Paralysed by grief, Joe silently slips out of the bathroom and sits on the floor beside me with a thud. I slowly turn my head to look at him; his eyes are red and his face pale. I open my mouth to speak, but I cry out at the thought of his name.

With the weight of the world on his shoulders, Joe runs his rough hands across his unshaven face.

"He has five scratches on his back that look like fingernail marks, with those awful black veins feeding into them. I'm guessing he was scratched by an Infected. I've seen bites before, and they look the same. I never knew you could get infected by a scratch."

Feeling sick to my stomach, I whisper, "But we don't

know that for sure, right? He could have got that from anywhere. He hasn't even left the walls. It doesn't make any sense. It must be a simple infection that…"

My voice fades as Joe stares at me with a solemn expression. Clearly frustrated, he quickly stands up and studies the gun in his hand. He murmurs in a broken voice, "Ally, it's over. All we need to do is figure out how to do this."

Sucking in a sharp breath, I shakily climb from my knees and beg.

"Please, you can't! He's my brother, Joe. He's doesn't deserve this! After all, we don't know for sure that he is infected! You said it yourself – you didn't even know that you could get infected from a scratch!"

Exacerbated, Joe throws up his arms. "He's infected, Ally, plain and simple – the sickness, the high temperature, the veins – everything is the same as a bite. If we tell the council what we know, they will kill him and chuck him over the walls like an animal! If we don't kill him ourselves, he's going to kill us, so what other option is there, huh? I have a duty to keep you safe!"

As despair overwhelms me, I push past Joe and enter the bathroom to see for myself. Tommy is still in the bathtub staring at the ceiling, breathing slow, rasping breaths. I lean over the tub to examine him and roll his shoulders forward to see the evidence for myself. Joe is right, there are five fingernail marks etched into the top of his back. The scratches are well and truly infected with the signature spidery black veins surrounding the wounds. With my heart in my throat, I kneel beside him.

"How did this happen? If you can hear me, please speak to me."

Tommy blinks as a single tear trickles down the side of his face. I bow my head in response and rest it on the edge of the bath. Joe stands rigidly next to the door, watching both of us like a hawk with his hand resting on his gun. Becoming agitated, he quickly grabs a towel, strides over to Tommy and lifts him out of the water. There are no more screams this time. He lies in Joe's arms, limp as a rag doll. I hadn't realised that I was holding my breath until the door closes behind them.

As I exhale loudly, my hands start to shake uncontrollably, so much so that it starts to make my teeth chatter in my head. I reach out to the wall for support as the familiar nightmarish images of my dead parents flash to the forefront of my mind, but this time they are not alone. Tommy is with them, reaching out for me with his rotten fingers and gangrene skin. Hyperventilating, I desperately try to blink away the images, but my anxiety only makes them stronger. Tommy's rotten, chomping mouth edges ever closer, frantic for my flesh.

Blinded by my own horrific imagination, I fumble for the bathroom door and practically fall into the lounge. This can't be the end for Tommy. We have worked too damn hard to survive this long. Buzzing with adrenaline and a belly full of fire, I storm into Tommy's room.

"We need to talk, Joe… NOW."

Placing Tommy back in his bed, he grabs me by the elbow and marches me back into the lounge.

I angrily rip my arm from his grasp. "You can't just make this huge decision for us. I know he's infected, and we need to be realistic, but—"

Joe's face flushes with anger. "There is no decision to be made! The end result is the same. He either dies a painful death from the infection, or we put him out of his misery. Do you really want him to suffer any more than he has already, Alyx? There is no cure, and there is only one way this story ends. He's dead already."

Joe's harsh words cut through me like fire and ice. Tommy will become one of them soon enough, and there's nothing either of us can do about it. My tears won't bring him back; my anger won't save him. My little brother is dying, and I can't do anything to save him. They try and teach it at school – being cold, hard, logical and ruthless – all in the name of fighting infection. But when it comes to killing your own little brother, it's not so damn easy. Funny how they leave that bit out.

As the bleak reality sinks into the pit of my stomach, Joe's expression softens a little.

"I love him like a son. I love both of you like you're my own, but we have to end it and on our terms, kid. This is what he would want. You go take a walk, and when I'm done, we can bury him together… have a funeral."

Numbness consumes me, making me feel like an empty void of nothingness. I somehow rigidly walk to the front door as Joe takes a step towards me.

"Don't you wanna say goodbye to him?"

Unable to look at him, I bow my head and grit my teeth through the pain.

"I just want to remember him as he was – my goofy, amazing, cheeky little brother. The way he made me smile when no one else could. I don't want to remember the thing that he is becoming now. If I see him now, I won't be able to leave and…" I take in a shuddery breath, "I won't let you end it."

20

Each step feels more painful and heavy with grief than the last. I sling the door wide open to find Will staring back at me; his face is flushed as he tries to catch his breath. At the sight of him, silent tears stream down my face, making me feel utterly wretched.

I whisper, "It's over. He's infected."

Grabbing my shoulder, he stares at me with fearful eyes. "I know he is, Ally… and they're coming for you."

SOMETIMES A SHOTGUN SPEAKS LOUDER THAN WORDS

Joe automatically launches into full army mode, grabs our survival packs and starts stuffing food into the pockets. I stand there barely functioning and unmoving. Taking my hand, Will drags me back into the house, slams the door behind us and pulls the heavy bolts across, securing it. The cogs begin to slowly turn in my clouded mind as I mumble, "I don't understand. Why do we need to leave? Surely we can reason with them?"

Joe calls out from the back of the house as he continues to prepare the weapons: "The council knows that Tommy has been unwell for a while, kid. When they examined him, they thought it was the flu or something because there were no bites. But now that they know he is infected, they will say we have been keeping him hidden, which is against the rules. They will kill him in the streets, and they will push us out as a warning to the rest of the folk. We'll have no weapons, no food, nothing… If we leave now, at least we stand a chance."

With utter dismay, I throw my arms up in the air. "But we didn't know either, Joe! How can they do that? And how do they even know that he's infected?"

Stopping in his tracks, he stares at me earnestly. "It doesn't matter how they know. It's already done. Maybe a friend of Tommy's knew and told someone… Who knows? But what I do know is that even if we kill Tommy this second, it still won't be enough. Trust me, I know these people, and I know what they do to people like me… people like us."

He continues to glare at me, waiting for a response. Pointing straight at Will he says, "I need you to tie up Tommy."

Will stands there wide-eyed. "You want me to tie him up?"

Joe shouts impatiently as he rushes into the bedroom, "There's rope out back. Grab a cloth to tie over his mouth!"

Will places his hand firmly on my shoulder. "You heard him – time to go, Ally!"

I wipe away the salty dampness from my cheeks with the back of my hand, as an overwhelming feeling of defiance and anger starts to spread through me. Gritting my teeth I clench my fists, digging my nails into the palms of my hands.

"I won't let them touch him…"

Will grins at me. "That's my girl!"

I dash forward, grab one of the survival packs and sling it over my shoulders. Will runs out back and returns with an armful of rope and a bandana hanging out of his pocket. Without a second thought, he goes straight into Tommy's bedroom and freezes at the sight of him. I nod knowingly and pull back the covers tangled around Tommy's legs. His pyjamas bottoms are still wet from his bath.

Will pulls at his legs and wraps the first rope around his ankles, pulling them tight. I hold Tommy's tiny wrists together in my hands as Will secures the final knots around his arms. He then hesitates with the bandana and briefly looks over his shoulder at me. Forcing a smile, I take it from his grasp and tie it around Tommy's face. He blinks in response with fearful eyes, as I lean over and kiss his forehead.

"Everything is going to be okay."

Will gently pulls me out of the way and places his hands underneath Tommy's arms. In one swift motion, he picks him up and slings him over his shoulder.

As he trudges towards the back door he shouts, "You owe me big time, Ally… I swear to god if he bites me, I'm gonna bite your ass too!"

I can't help but smirk at the thought of it. The townsfolk finally arrive outside the front of the cabin and immediately begin to slam their fists on the front door, bellowing for us to come out. At the front of the crowd is the father of one of Tommy's closest friends. Joe opens his mouth to speak as his handmade window smashes, showering him in glass. I dash forward and flip the dining table in response, quickly pushing it towards the broken window. Joe grabs a shotgun off the wall and cocks it with one hand.

"THAT'S IT! No one smashes a window in my house! You two take Tommy. I'll hold them off and meet you down by the river, okay?"

I nod my head furiously as Joe pulls me in for a tight hug, kissing the top of my head.

"Be safe, kid."

He hands me the pistol tucked into his belt and looks at me with wild eyes.

"Remember everything I taught you and you'll be fine, okay? This is just in case, for Tommy."

Swallowing my fear, I shove the pistol into my belt loop, and with a rucksack on each shoulder now, I draw my sword, readying myself for what lies ahead. As he releases the table, a mass of bodies fall into the house through the window. Joe points his gun into the oncoming crowd.

"I give you three seconds to get outta my house or I'll blow your god damn heads off!"

That ought to keep them occupied. With that, Will and I race out the back door without looking back. As we scramble through the gardens, Will slings Tommy over his right shoulder, unable to continue carrying him as he was. Rather worryingly, Tommy doesn't even let out a moan at being flung around by Will. Uncertain of how we are going to get out of the town walls, I quickly realise there's no way we can climb over the walls with Tommy. The only feasible way out is through the gate, which is manned by soldiers.

Changing direction from the usual place that we enter the forest, we sprint ahead through the dusty streets. Will strains, visibly gritting his teeth as he huffs along with Tommy.

"We're going for the gate aren't we, Ally? Because there's no way I can drag Tommy over the wall!"

I offer to carry Tommy, but Will refuses and pushes on. With the gate in view now, a young soldier appears to be confused by our presence and even more confused when he sees Tommy tied up and being carried by Will. I shove my sword into my belt and pull out the gun, steadying myself and taking aim at the soldier's head.

"Open the gate!"

Startled by my demand, the soldier quickly gathers his thoughts and attempts to dissipate the situation.

"Now listen, you know I can't do that! You need an official—"

"I said, open the gate!"

I click the safety off and stare down the idiot soldier; he's clearly a newbie as his eyes widen at my retort. He opens and closes his mouth like a fish, uncertain of what he should be doing.

With my patience quickly fading, I continue to glare at him.

"Look, douche bag, we both know there are no Infected on the other side of the gate. Just let us through and no one gets hurt, okay!"

The newbie's hands start shaking as he stiffly walks to the gate and pulls back the heavy bolts. The loud creaking noise attracts other more experienced soldiers in a nearby watchtower. Before they can stop us, Will and I squeeze through the tiny gap and sprint towards the forest edge.

As soon as we make the safety of the trees, Will collapses with Tommy in his arms. Sweat pours down his face as he desperately tries to catch his breath. Taking Tommy from Will's arms, I prop him up against a tree and pull down the bandana from his mouth. His skin feels cold and clammy to the touch; he doesn't have much time. Will continues to lie on the floor, exhausted, and rubs his biceps.

Leaning over towards him, I say, "Thank you. I couldn't have done this without you."

He shrugs his shoulders. "Nah, it's nothing. You would have done the same for me. Nothing like a bit of exercise in the afternoon."

His cheeky grin falls from his face when he sees Tommy's colour.

"He doesn't look so good, Ally. We don't want to linger too long. We're pretty exposed here."

I nod my head, feeling sick to my stomach. If Joe doesn't meet us soon, I'm going to have to do this. The thought of pulling the trigger makes my head swim. How could I find the strength to do this? How could I kill my brother? I'm not sure I can. I sling the rucksacks on the floor and shakily kneel in front of Tommy, pulling the bandana slowly back over his mouth.

I put my hand behind Tommy's shoulder to lift him, but Will quickly puts his hand out. "Let me, Ally. It's okay."

I am a little relieved as Will picks Tommy up once again and starts to trudge deeper into the forest. I take one final glance at the wall and wonder what the future will bring for Joe and me. Hopefully something safer than this place – well, as safe as you can get these days. As I follow Will and head for the river, a lump begins to rise in my throat as I realise that whatever happens, our future doesn't include Tommy anymore, all because of one little scratch.

After thirty minutes of trekking, we reach the river, amazingly without running into any Infected: at least something has gone our way today. Will gently places Tommy on the ground against a tree. Sitting down heavily, he exhales loudly as he runs his fingers through his sandy hair. With an overwhelming sense of dread, I suddenly become very aware of the feel of Joe's gun on my hip. I look to Tommy, who seems to be barely breathing now.

Unable to sit, I start to pace back and forth, willing myself to have the courage to do this.

Seeing my anxiety, Will croaks, "I can't even imagine what you are feeling right now, and I don't know if this will help you, but I would just focus on how much worse it would be if you saw him as one of them."

Tears begin to flow down my face again; I don't even attempt to wipe them away this time. Seeing my distraught expression, he quickly jumps to his feet and holds his hand out.

"Go take a walk."

Will's offer instantly makes me stop pacing. I stare at Tommy's boyish face and memorise the curve of his nose and his angular jaw. I love him so much it makes my heart ache. I bite my bottom lip so hard that the taste of copper starts to trickle into my mouth.

I murmur under my breath, "No. It should be me."

I close my eyes and focus on steadying my own breathing. Joe's military training runs through my head as a feeling of coldness begins to spread through me. I open my eyes and stifle back a sob; Tommy's chest appears to be still. Amazingly his sallow cheeks look almost porcelain now as the sun starts to dip behind the trees. I mechanically feel for the cold, hard gun holstered on my hip.

I'm aware that Will is speaking to me hurriedly, but all I can hear is my own heartbeat pounding in my ears. Everything slows down. The gun feels even heavier in my hands than it did earlier as I click the safety off once more. As I stiffly raise my arm and point the gun to Tommy's forehead, for a fleeting moment, memories of us together flash through the forefront of my mind. Like a flipbook of photos, they are gone before I can even register them. Closing my eyes I hold my arm perfectly still, unable to look at the consequences of my bullet.

A silent tear falls down my face as I whisper, "I love you, Tommy."

As I pull down my finger and apply pressure on the trigger, the breath is knocked out of my lungs. A searing pain explodes in my head as the sound of Will's muffled cries fills my ears. Unable to fight it, and desperate to stay awake, a shroud of darkness suddenly overwhelms me, sending me into a black hole of unconsciousness.

BACK FROM THE DEAD

I open my eyes to see the canopy of the trees swaying overhead. The sun has nearly set behind them now as the cool forest floor begins to chill my bones. Blinking hard, I try to clear my clouded mind. Am I alive? Is Tommy dead? In the distance, I can faintly hear voices laughing and joking. Feeling anxious, I try to prop myself up, but my head starts to throb with every movement.

Reaching up, I touch my forehead to find a wet, cold sock glued to my face. Feeling completely grossed out, I hope that it's clean. Footsteps quickly make their way over to me as I wince in pain. Will's head pops into view, as I steadily lay back down on the forest floor.

"Hey, sleepy head! You've been out cold for a while."

Looking over his shoulder, he grins at someone out of view.

"Someone's here to see you!"

More footsteps hurriedly make their way over to me as I try to steady my breathing. Tommy suddenly leans over and smiles at me, grinning from ear to ear. His light chocolate eyes twinkle in the dim evening hue.

"Thanks for not shooting me, sis!"

In shock, I sit up, ignoring the throbbing pain in my

head, and grab his face, studying it. "How is this possible? You were dead, I saw you die… And the scratch! You were Infected! This can't be true. I must be dreaming, right? Or am I dead? But if I'm dead, why is Will here?"

Tommy's laugh is like music to my ears as he looks over to Will.

"Honestly, Ally, I don't know what happened! One minute I felt the sickest I have ever felt in my life. Then I fell asleep, but it felt different from normal sleep. Then I woke up feeling amazing and saw you lying face down on the ground! Thankfully Will stopped you from shooting me, but you hit your head pretty hard and passed out… Oh, and the sock on your face was Will's idea."

My mind whirls as I try to understand everything. "But how can you go from being supposedly infected one second to completely cured the next?"

He shrugs his shoulders. "I have no idea. I really don't."

My head begins to thump even more, making me feel a little nauseated. I peel the sock off my forehead and inspect it.

"I'm not even going to ask if this thing is clean!"

Grinning at me, Tommy leans in and quickly pulls me into a hug. He whispers in my ear, "Thanks for believing in me, Ally. You brought me back from the dead."

Releasing me from his strong grip, he kisses me on the cheek and smiles. In awe, I reach up and touch Tommy's soft cheek; his skin is utterly flawless, and his usually flat, listless hair is now lustrous and glossy. In that moment, I realised he looks strikingly beautiful, more than he ever did before he became sick. The stark contrast from his deathly appearance barely an hour ago, to this, is so astounding that I find it difficult to process.

With my mind spinning, I turn to Will to find out what I missed.

"You must have seen something, Will? Tommy died! His chest wasn't moving… or at least I thought it wasn't. The last thing I remember is hearing your muffled voice?"

Shaking his head and speaking quickly, he answers, "Didn't you hear me speak to you? You raised your arm as he started to do this weird morphing thing. I didn't know exactly what was happening, but I did know that he wasn't turning. It just happened so quickly, and before I knew it, you were aiming the gun at his head, and you couldn't hear anything that I was saying to you. So, the only thing I could do was take you down… Sorry about that."

Closing my eyes in disbelief, it seems too crazy to be true, but then again, we live in a world where the dead come back to life. I guess anything is possible. Trying to reassure myself that this isn't some crazy dream, I ask, "So how do you feel, Tommy?"

Barely able to contain his smile, he says, "I feel awesome! Frikkin awesome! The scratches on my back have pretty much gone, and I feel almost electric, like I never need to sleep."

Tommy lifts his shirt up to expose his back. The scratches that were oozing pus have almost disappeared. The only evidence of any wound is five silver lines that are paler than his milky skin tone. Just as I open my mouth to question Tommy on how he got those damn scratches in the first place, he suddenly stands up and points his face into the wind.

With a look of confusion on his face, he mutters, "I think Joe's coming?"

I instantly stand up and stare into the distance, desperately hoping that he isn't hurt. When I realise that he is nowhere to be seen, I furrow my brow at Tommy.

"Hang on, you said you *think* he's coming?"

Pointing ahead, he says, "I know it sounds weird, but I can hear footsteps and can kind of smell him."

Slack-jawed, I wonder if Tommy is some kind of monster. "How can you possibly know that?"

Tommy opens his mouth to respond, but I hold my hand up to stifle his response. Utterly disturbed, I start to pace back and forth.

"Okay, so let me get this straight. One minute you're infected and you're going to turn, next minute you're alive, looking amazing and can hear when someone is coming… oh, and you can smell them too? Okay, that's totally normal!"

Tommy's eyes instantly widen at my outburst as the gravity of the situation begins to dawn on him. Dropping his gaze, he studies his hands and his bottom lip begins to tremble. He suddenly crosses his arms over his chest defensively and stares at the ground, trying to avoid eye contact. Feeling as though I have stepped too far, I open my arms and pull Tommy in for another protective embrace and try to ignore the sense of dread gnawing in the pit of my stomach.

"Tommy, I'm so sorry! I didn't mean to frighten you. When I told you that everything would be okay, I meant it! You're alive. Nothing else matters right now. We'll figure out what this all means later."

He buries his head into the hollow of my neck and squeezes me so tightly that he cracks my back. I quickly realise that the muscles in his chest are rock hard, not like his soft pre-teen former self. I try to push away from the painful hug.

"Tommy, you're kinda hurting me!"

A little embarrassed, he quickly lets go, looking at me sheepishly. "Sorry, I guess I don't know my own strength."

As I stare at Tommy with his perfect porcelain skin and long, glossy brown hair, my mind is a whirlwind of emotions; a part of me still can't believe this is happening. Maybe miracles do exist, or maybe Tommy is the cure for infection. The very thought sends a chill down my spine.

All those people that have died, potentially murdered, who could have been saved. I try to push away these dark thoughts and focus on the here and now. I have my little brother back; my prayers have been answered. With our future so uncertain, I have to live in the moment and enjoy it while it lasts because something tells me that our journey is far from over.

THE STARVING ANIMAL

We all stand in awkward silence, waiting for Joe to arrive. Tommy continues to stand there with his arms folded across his chest looking anxious, and for the first time in my life, it appears that Will is utterly speechless. Barely an hour ago my little brother somehow managed to survive infection and now seems to have new superhuman abilities as a result of it. Amazingly, and rather worryingly, he believes that he can both hear and smell Joe approaching through the forest, even though Joe is nowhere to be seen.

Thinking ahead, I didn't want to overwhelm Joe too much, therefore I quickly asked Tommy to stay hidden before he arrives. A part of me hopes that Tommy is wrong, that he has imagined these new abilities and that maybe he was never infected in the first place. But as I stare at his perfect complexion and muscular form, I know deep down that it is probably true. Either way, all I can hope is that we find some answers soon.

To my relief, Joe suddenly appears and almost stumbles through the underbrush; he looks a little dishevelled with a torn shirt and mud on his knees, but otherwise is completely unharmed. He pauses at a nearby tree and leans heavily against it with flushed cheeks, wiping the back of his hand across his brow. Swallowing back my own fear, I try to focus on breaking the news rather than processing the implications of Tommy's new abilities. As Joe continues to catch his breath, I race over and place my hand on the small of his back.

"Are you okay?"

Straightening his stance, he nods his head. "I'm fine, kiddo… Seems I ain't as fit as I used to be."

Will takes a step towards us. "Glad you got out in one piece."

Joe smiles and raises his eyebrows. "Can't say the same about those assholes that broke my windows!"

Will and I exchange a glance, uncertain of how to present the now-cured Tommy.

Immediately spotting the exchange, Joe is instantly on guard.

"What's going on, kid? Where's Tommy?"

You can't get anything past him. Without saying a word, I simply turn around and beckon for Tommy to join us. Hesitating at first, he tentatively steps out from behind a large tree and slowly walks towards us. At the sight of him, Joe's face completely drains of colour, almost as though he has seen a ghost.

He whispers under his breath, "Tommy? How can this be?"

Tommy laughs nervously. "Hey, Joe… guess I'm back from the dead?"

Joe quickly reaches forward, pulls him in for a long hug and slaps him on the back. He grabs Tommy's face with his huge, rough hands and speaks in a wavering voice: "I'm so sorry, kid. I damn well thought you were infected. If it weren't for Alyx…"

He bows his head ashamedly and sighs heavily.

"It doesn't matter. You're here now, and that's all that matters."

Joe smiles with watery eyes and wraps his arm around Tommy's shoulder, looking the happiest I have ever seen him in my life.

"We don't wanna linger here for too long, kids, but we have enough time for a little celebration. I think we all deserve it, huh?"

As I stare at them both, my heart swells with love. My little family is back together again with my best friend at my side. In this moment, I feel like I could be the luckiest girl in the world.

Joe winks at me with glistening eyes.

"So, Ally, crack open the champagne!"

I roll my eyes at him. "No champagne I'm afraid, but I may have something we can eat?"

I reach down into my rucksack and start to pull out the food that Joe packed from the cupboards – cheese, bread, dried beef, apples and a bag of homemade sweet biscuits. Considering the situation, and the fact we were run out of town, I think we did okay. Tommy automatically snatches some of the dried beef from my hand and starts gnawing on it hungrily. Stunned by his actions, I cautiously reach forward.

"Take it easy, Tommy. That's got to last us."

He jerks away from me, almost defending his food, and continues to chew on it ravenously. Between mouthfuls he says, "I'm just so hungry it hurts!"

Joe raises his chin and narrows his eyes. "It's okay, kid. You take a seat, and we'll sort out some food for you."

Tommy scurries away and crouches on the floor in an

awkward position; he is so focused on eating the dried meat that he barely stops to take a breath. Joe momentarily looks at me out of the corner of his eye, and exhales quietly before rubbing his hands over his unshaven face.

Understanding his anxiety, I attempt to ease the tension in the group by focusing on distributing the food. I rigidly bend down and start ripping the bread into four sizeable chunks and quickly pass a piece to Joe. As soon as our eyes meet, I give him a strained smile, something that my mum used to do in uncomfortable situations.

Will leans against a tree and holds his hand out blindly before taking his portion from me. With his jaw set firmly, he rips off a corner of the white soft bread and pops it into his mouth, as he continues to watch Tommy closely. With nothing left to do, I start to mechanically eat my own portion of bread without even really tasting it.

Even though I have barely eaten today, watching Tommy tear apart the remnants of his dried meat like a starving animal is starting to make my hunger disappear. Joe kneels down and places a hand gently on the small of Tommy's back, and holds out a chunk of bread for him.

"Here you go, kid. Now take your time. I know you must be hungry after all the sickness, but if you eat too quickly, you will probably throw it up again, okay?"

Ignoring him, Tommy grabs the bread and shoves the whole thing into his mouth. With barely any room to breathe, he starts to dribble white bready goo down his chin. After swallowing it practically whole, he suddenly looks up at me with wild eyes desperate for more food. Without thinking, and completely in shock, I automatically offer him my half-eaten chunk of bread;

he snatches it from my grasp and immediately shoves it into his mouth.

Noting my horror, Will reaches out and presents half of his portion of bread to me, probably to try and distract me from the scene unfolding in front of us. I smile grimly, thank him and shake my head. Unable to watch Tommy any longer, I decide I need some space.

"I need to pee. Be back in a minute…"

Joe seizes the opportunity. "I'll go with you, kid. I don't want you wandering off out here by yourself."

Before we leave, Joe gestures towards Tommy. "Will, can you…"

His voice fades before he finishes his sentence. Will holds up his hand and smiles at him reassuringly. Joe nods at him gratefully and turns to follow me into the woods. The tension in the air is palpable as we walk side by side without so much as glancing at each other. Once far enough away from Tommy and Will, I open my mouth to speak, but Joe stops me in my path and clamps his hand down on my shoulder.

"Whatever it is you're about to say, just hold it. Until we know what we are dealing with here, we just need to support Tommy but be on guard at the same time. Just because he's alive, we can't be complacent."

I nod my head slowly and hiss through my teeth, "Amongst everything else, he now has an amazing sense of hearing! He said he heard you coming before you even got here, and he said he could smell you too!"

Joe exhales and reflexively grabs for his cigarettes in his pocket. As soon as he lights up, he takes a long drag and stares at me determinedly.

"Right now, all we need to do is focus on finding somewhere to camp for the night and trying to survive."

I try to swallow, but the remnants of the bread make it incredibly difficult. With a sense of doubt fluttering in my tummy, and a million unanswerable questions racing through my mind, I'm uncertain of how to respond without revealing too much. Chewing my lip nervously, I say the only thing that I know I can say.

"I love you, Joe, you know that right?"

He smiles at me with sad eyes and ruffles my hair. "Go on, you dope, go pee! Otherwise, when we get back, you will actually need to pee!"

With that, I make my way through the bushes for some privacy and commence the undignified squat that girls have to do in these embarrassing situations. Being a guy must be so much easier sometimes. We make our way back to find Tommy slumped against a tree, clutching his stomach and groaning in pain.

"My tummy hurts, big time!"

Joe bends down to examine him. "Well, kid, I'm not surprised! You haven't eaten properly in days, so your stomach has probably shrunk a little, and shoving that food down was probably a bit much."

Tommy groans again in response. "I just couldn't stop myself, and what's worse is that I could probably eat more right now!"

Will interjects, "Well, I'm no doctor, but I'm pretty sure if you eat anything else, you will puke for sure."

Tommy frowns a little. "I think I've done enough puking in the last seventy-two hours to last a lifetime."

Joe stands without taking his eyes off Tommy. "Well, we

need to find a place to camp for the night, and we are losing light rapidly. Maybe a gentle walk will help you digest all that food?"

Still clutching his stomach, Tommy stands and leans against a tree, grimacing in pain. Will gestures forward and smiles at him, encouraging him to start walking up front. Tommy bows his head sulkily in response and momentarily stares at me with his puppy-dog eyes before slowly stomping through the trees into the unknown. As soon as his back is turned, Will gently places his hand on the hilt of his sword and narrows his focus. He follows closely behind, watching every single movement.

We eventually find a small clearing in the woods with a mixture of large breeze blocks and bricks in the centre; at some point in the past, this probably used to resemble a house. With the darkness looming, we are running out of options for a suitable camp site for the night, and although we have no place to hide here, we will have an excellent vantage point against any Infected.

Testing to see that the bricks are safe, Joe starts to climb to the top and pushes the rocks as he goes. Meanwhile, Will investigates the perimeter for any animal traps; the last thing we need is to get caught in a trap when trying to escape the Infected in the cover of darkness. Both Will and Joe agree that the location is a suitable resting place, or in reality, the best that we are going to find out here in the wilderness at dusk.

Placing my sword in my belt, I start to climb to the top of the boulders and wonder what our chances are of surviving out here. If we don't meet any Infected tonight, it will be nothing short of a miracle, and given how the rest of this day has turned out, I think it's pretty damn likely. At the top, I sling my rucksack on the floor and lean against it, feeling exhausted. Joe quickly riffles through his army survival kit and starts to pull out its contents, examining them. Putting on some gloves, he starts to unravel the sharp trip wire and clips small silver bells to it, along with tiny colourful flags.

They say that the Infected have terrible eyesight and are mostly driven by their other senses. During his tour in the military, Joe saw an Infected that had no eyes but somehow still managed to function. Although the wire would not stop the Infected altogether, it would alert us to their location and maybe slow them down a little. Out here, that would at least give us a fighting chance of surviving the night.

Putting some socks over his hands, Will waits for Joe at the bottom and grabs the other end of the wire. Still clutching his stomach, Tommy curls up against me and groans in pain.

With watery frightened eyes, he stares up at me.

"What's happening to me, Ally? I'm scared."

I pull him towards me, letting him rest his head on my shoulder.

"I don't know, Tommy. I really don't. But one thing I can promise you is that I will die before I let anything else happen to you, okay? You're alive. That's all that matters."

Looking up at me, he smiles grimly and then places his head on my shoulder once more. As I exhale quietly and give Tommy a gentle squeeze to comfort him, we watch Will and Joe rig up the trip wire amongst the trees in silence. Once finished, a very tired Will and Joe climb back up to the top of the boulders to join us for the night.

Will takes a seat next to me as Joe starts to pace back and forth, clearly agitated.

"Okay, guys, you know how it usually works – two sleep and two keep watch. But Tommy needs to rest to make sure he's fit for our hike tomorrow."

Tommy suddenly sits up with a pouty, angry expression on his face.

"I don't need to sleep. I'm fine!"

Joe holds up his hands. "Even so, Tommy, the last few days you damn well nearly died! Even if you don't need to sleep, you can rest, okay?"

Tommy huffs and crosses his arms over his chest. He may have some bizarre new powers, if that's what you want to call them, but Tommy is still a teenager.

Joe continues, almost stumbling over his words, "Okay, so I'll sleep first while it's still relatively light, and you both keep watch until eleven. Then, Will and I keep watch until three, and Ally gets her head down. Then we wake up Ally and Will sleeps until morning... got it?"

Will shrugs his shoulders. "Yeah, just give me a shout when it's my turn to crash. Luckily for me, I can sleep standing up!"

Joe says wearily, "I don't think I'm gonna have trouble having a kip. I'm getting too old for all this."

With that, Joe slowly sits on the floor, leans against a rock opposite us and feels for his cigarette pouch. As soon as he examines its contents, he quickly realises that like everything, he needs to ration them now.

Crossing his arms over his chest, he shoves the pouch back into his pocket and looks to Tommy. "Well, kid, I think I can speak for everyone here when I say how happy

I am that you're alive… but you need to tell us what happened."

Tommy visibly swallows and looks to me for reassurance, but I shrug my shoulders in response. "Don't look at me. I'm with Joe on this one – we deserve an explanation."

Accepting defeat, he sits forward and fiddles with his trouser leg nervously. With bated breath, we listen intently as Tommy explains how he became scratched.

THE SCRATCH

Tommy continues to fidget as he opens and closes his mouth like a fish; he clearly doesn't know how to begin his story. The fact that he is hesitating so much leads me to believe that he did something stupid. With Joe becoming impatient, I hold my hand out to Tommy. Taking his small hands in mine, I stare at him earnestly.

"No one is mad at you, Tommy. We just need to know the truth."

Tommy exhales loudly and focuses his thoughts, before addressing Joe with a guilty expression.

"Well, it was last Sunday, and I was hanging out with Ed, Jace and Stu. We were kinda bored, so we thought it might be cool to check out the doc's lab…"

I furrow my brow at him. "Really, Tommy? Breaking and entering? What's wrong with you?"

"Oh yeah?" he replied defensively. "What about you and your boyfriend's adventures outside the walls every five minutes!"

Joe gives me a warning look as I open my mouth to snap back. We need to figure out what happened, and now is not the time to bicker. Swallowing my pride and biting my tongue, I reluctantly gesture for Tommy to continue with his story.

"I know we shouldn't have broken in, but we did. So, we managed to get into Artie's lab pretty easily, and he has a ton of medicine stashed! Even though he always says that we are running out and makes everyone use herbal alternatives."

Arthur Dunlop, who works in the lab as the town's only doctor, is one of my favourite people. Even though he is in huge demand and under an awful amount of pressure, he always takes the time to ask how you are and then tells you a cheesy joke. With his positive disposition and huge white beard, he reminds me of a skinny Father Christmas. Basically, he's one of the last people you would ever think of as putting lives at risk.

My automatic response is to defend Arthur, thinking that maybe he's just being cautious, but he could be the reason that Tommy almost died. I have a feeling that whatever Tommy is about to tell me may change my opinion on Arthur.

"We get into the lab and find an Infected strapped to a metal trolley in a small room near the main lab. This thing has all kinds of tubes, wires and monitors attached to it. At first, we thought that it was dead because it wasn't moving or chomping, so I went in for a closer look…"

Sucking in a sharp breath, I clench my fists, turning my knuckles white. Joe's face flushes bright red as he grinds his teeth at Tommy. Noting the tension, Tommy almost stumbles over his words to justify his actions.

"I know it was stupid, but I have never seen an Infected up close before! The thing suddenly woke up, and I thought that the straps were tighter than they were. It lunged forward, grabbed my shirt and pulled me towards its mouth. Stupid thing nearly took a chunk out of my neck. Luckily

46

Ed pulled me free, and we got the hell out of there! At the time, I hadn't realised that it had scratched me until I got home…"

Tommy hangs his head in shame as Joe swallows his anger and clenches his jaw.

"This Infected, what did it look like? Anyone we know from town?"

Tommy shakes his head. "Its eyes were all sunken, and half of its face was missing. All you could see were rotten teeth and exposed bones mostly. I have no idea who that thing used to be."

Will, who until this point had been very quiet, suddenly speaks. "Whatever drugs Arthur gave to that thing could be the reason why you didn't turn. Maybe he was trying to find a cure? Or maybe he was trying to do something more sinister, hence the abilities. Guess there's no way of knowing."

Tommy visibly swallows as his eyes suddenly become watery. "But what if the drugs wear off and I become infected?"

Will reaches out and places his hand on Tommy's shoulder. "To be honest, we need to be prepared for that. We don't know what we are dealing with here."

I pull Tommy in for a defensive hug and simultaneously give Will a warning look at the thought of the infection taking him away. Trying to comfort Tommy, I say, "We don't know what will happen – maybe nothing, maybe something. Just try not to worry about it. I think we should be more concerned about a horde of Infected coming for us in the night."

Joe nods his head thoughtfully and responds in a gruff

voice, "She's right, kid. In an ideal world, we would go back to town and get some damn answers from Arthur, but that's too risky. If we go back, they will probably shoot us all dead before we get anywhere near the gates."

We all nod our head in agreement as Joe continues, "I have a friend who I served in the military with who might be able to help us, someone we can trust. The last I heard, she was in the capital, Alhena. She may be long gone, but I guess it's our best shot. We can head for the capital in the morning, but right now I gotta get my head down."

Joe hands his automatic shotgun to Will. "Ever used one of these, buddy?"

Will shakes his head as he examines it. "No, but I'm sure I can figure it out."

Joe moves his rucksack and lies down. He puts his head on his bag and folds his arms across his chest.

"Just remember, it's no good at a distance. It's for when they get up close and personal, okay, kid?"

He holds the gun firmly against his shoulder and grins to himself. "Okay, cool. Thanks."

Seeming satisfied, Joe shuts his eyes as Will and I prepare for our watch duty. Tommy also tries to sneakily leave with us, but without even opening his eyes Joe says, "Stay where you are, Tommy! Remember what I said, you need your rest!"

Tommy huffs and sulkily sits back on the ground, crossing his legs. Giving him a crooked smile, Will says, "See ya, Tommy!"

Taking one last look at my brother's pouty face, I sigh and start to make my way down the boulders once more. At the bottom, Will is slightly ahead and holds his hand out for me to help me down. Still feeling a little mad at him, I ignore his gesture and stomp past him, heading for the trees. Dropping his hand by his side, he stares at me intensely.

"Look, I know what I said has upset you, but I was only telling the truth, Alyx."

I spin around to confront him. "I know, Will. I know, okay! He's just a kid! Don't you think he's been through enough already without making him worry about what *might* happen?"

Will holds up his hands.

"I'm sorry, but I think you're wrong. He's not 'just a kid', Alyx. I think he deserves to know about this kind of stuff. At the end of the day, he could still turn at any moment! So, we all need to be prepared, including Tommy."

Not wanting to admit it, I know Will is right; Tommy isn't a kid anymore, and the reality is he could turn at any moment. But he's my little brother and always will be. Feeling tired and irritable, I realise that none of it matters anyway. It's done, and we have bigger problems. Like the hordes of Infected in this forest.

I storm past him. "You know, Will, sometimes a little bit of sensitivity goes a long way!" Before I reach the tree line I hiss, "Oh, and by the way, don't call me Alyx! I hate it when you call me that!"

Raising his eyebrows, he whispers under his breath, "Sheesh… this is gonna be a long night!"

Cocking his shotgun, Will follows me into the darkening forest.

Two hours into sentry duty, the forest is almost entirely dark. Fortunately, the sky is clear tonight and the moon is casting welcome slivers of light between the trees. With my eyes adjusting to the darkness, I stand stonily still, straining to hear any Infected. Luckily, the only thing I can hear at the moment is a chorus of crickets.

Will and I haven't spoken since our argument, so we've been walking the perimeter in complete silence, partly because we don't want to attract any Infected by making any unnecessary noise, and partly because we're both still seething. The thing is, Will and I almost never argue, but when we do, we're both pretty damn stubborn.

Will suddenly stops behind me, quickly drawing his sword. The clink of the metal sends me into high alert as I spin around and draw my own sword. I carefully pace towards him as he stares at something in the distance.

He narrows his focus. "Did you just see that?"

Taking a step forward, I look to where he is pointing and squint my eyes. I try to focus in the darkness, but I can't see anything. Still vibrating with adrenaline, I blindly start to tiptoe forward with Will close by my side. As we go further and further away from the safety of the perimeter, Will slows his pace and starts to search in other directions.

Clutching my sword tightly I hiss, "What the hell are we looking for? Is it an Infected?"

Whispering hurriedly, he replies, "I think I saw someone…a girl with white hair. I'm pretty sure she was human and not an Infected."

I'm shocked that there may be other people in the woods at this time of night.

"Are you sure? How old was she, a little girl or—"

He shakes his head. "Not young, probably a teenager. I only saw her for a second."

"Let's keep looking then."

"No, let's keep walking the perimeter. We can't leave Joe and Tommy unprotected. If we see her again, we should corner her then."

I become more and more anxious. "But if she's dangerous, shouldn't we be hunting her down right now?"

Will turns around and starts to peer into the distance agitatedly. Living in a walled community gives you a false sense of security; sometimes other people can be as dangerous as the Infected. Feeling helpless, I stare into Will's round green eyes and suddenly wish that we were back at home, not standing here in the forest with our lives at stake. Every decision we make now will mean that we either survive or die.

Taking a step closer, I reach out and place my hand on his wrist.

"We gotta wake them up…"

Understanding that we have no other option, he nods in agreement. After all, we can't run after this girl and leave Joe and Tommy exposed to the Infected. We need to inform Joe as he may have other priorities. Still gripping my sword tightly, we stealthily make our way back to camp.

Trying to make light of the situation, Will grins.

"Well, at least you're talking to me now."

Rolling my eyes at him, I stomp ahead. "I wouldn't be surprised if you imagined this girl anyway!"

Even though I can't see his face, I can feel him smirking behind my back. As we approach the boulders, Tommy is standing at the top with a hardened expression staring down at us. Joe is out of sight and must be sleeping. I feel bad about waking Joe as he's been through so much, but we have no other option. Besides, he would be seriously mad if something did happen and we hadn't woken him.

When I reach the top, I find Joe lying on the ground as we left him. I walk over quietly to him and gently place my hand on his forearm. Not wanting to startle him, I whisper, "Joe… Wake up!"

His eyes fling open as he suddenly sits up and grabs for his sword. Trying to calm him, I hold up my hands.

"Everything is fine. We're okay."

Exhaling with relief, he rubs his hand across his stubbly chin. Bewildered, he looks at his surroundings as he croaks, "I guess it's my watch already. Feel like I've been asleep for five minutes."

I glance over my shoulder at Will before answering Joe.

"No, it's not your watch yet, but we have a situation."

As soon as the words leave my mouth, he jumps to his feet.

"What kind of situation?"

Gesturing towards Will, I say, "Will saw a girl in the woods, and she wasn't infected. We thought you should know."

Now fully awake and in soldier mode, Joe's mind visibly races as he furrows his brow.

"Right, Will, I want every last detail. How old was she? Was she armed? What did she look like?"

Will stares into the distance. "She was a teenager, probably sixteen or seventeen. I didn't see any weapon, but that's not to say that she didn't have one… She had white hair and pale skin. Sorry, Joe. I only saw her for a second, and then she was gone!"

Joe begins to process Will's information and runs his fingers through his hair with frustration.

"What was she wearing? Was she in rags or military gear? Try and think, Will. Any details could help us right now."

Shrugging his shoulders, Will replies, "As I say, I only saw her for a second, so I couldn't say for sure. Plus, it's pretty damn dark out there."

Joe places his hand on Will's shoulder. "It's okay, kid. You did the right thing."

He paces to the edge of the rock and peers into the forest. "When I was in the military, we would often come across wild folk that lived out in the forests. Most of them were savages and rejected walled communities like Merope. Sometimes they hunt in packs and sometimes they hunt on their own. So, this girl you saw is probably one of those people, and I can guarantee that she will be a force to be reckoned with. She will know these woods like the back of her hand and doesn't need the sun to navigate her way. To be honest, she's probably watching us right now…"

As I try to steady my breathing, all the hairs stand up on the back of my neck.

"So, what you're saying, Joe, is that this girl could probably kill us all in a heartbeat?"

He nods his head.

"And just because we saw her on her own, doesn't mean that she's alone. There could be others."

I try to swallow, but my mouth has become dry. "So, what do we do?"

Joe paces to the other side of the rock and peers into the darkness.

"We all stay up here – no more walking the perimeter. We wait it out until sunrise, and then we haul ass to the nearest walled town."

Rolling a cigarette, he continues, "Now that I am awake, you should get your head down, Ally, if you can."

I look at him warily. "Well, with the combination of wild teenage assassins and the Infected, I think getting my head down is unlikely!"

He reaches out and pats my shoulder. "You never know, kid. You might surprise yourself."

Feeling resigned, I realise that even if I can't sleep, which is highly probable, I can try and rest as much as possible. I crawl over to where Joe's rucksack is on the floor and lay my head on his bag. I zip up my woollen jacket and pull the hood up over my face.

With my eyes closed, I feel Tommy creep in beside me and snuggle into the nook of my shoulder. When we were kids, after our mum and dad died, Joe would often find us just like this, snuggled up in the same bed together. Growing up in a world where monsters really could be hiding under the bed meant that sleeping as a kid was never easy. Being on constant alert became so ingrained that I can't remember the last time I slept deeply. Tommy breathes out, blowing warm air into the side of my neck, and I can't help but smile at the memory of us being kids.

I tilt my head and whisper to him, "You probably don't remember, but when we were young, Mum used to sing to us to try and get us to sleep."

As I cast my mind back to my mum's soft singing, I can almost smell her perfume on the underside of her wrist as she lovingly stroked our hair. Without even realising I start to recall the song:

"How much is that doggy in the window?
The one with the waggly tail
How much is that doggy in the window?
I do hope that he is for sale…"

Before I can finish the song, Tommy and I drift into a dream-filled sleep, smiling at the lasting image of our mother's warm serenity.

ALWAYS TRUST YOUR INSTINCTS

In the early hours of the morning, Will gently shakes my shoulder and whispers something inaudible. Not wanting to wake up, I reluctantly blink away the blurriness of sleep from my eyes as I begin to adjust to my surroundings. With my eyes fully open, I am suddenly confronted by Will's face leaning over me as he stifles a yawn.

"Morning…"

The moonlight shines through his golden hair as he brushes an errant strand impatiently out of his glistening green eyes. Tommy suddenly sits bolt upright and jumps to his feet. In an attempt to steady himself, he puts his hands on his hips and looks a little dazed.

Will continues, "If you don't get up soon, I'm gonna need matchsticks to keep my eyes open!"

Rubbing my dead shoulder, I exhale as I sit up. "Okay, okay, I'm getting up…"

By the time I'm standing, Will is already lying on Joe's rucksack. Pulling his hood up around his face, he smirks.

"Thanks for keeping it warm for me!"

Relaxing his shoulders, he closes his eyes, and within minutes he's fast asleep.

I turn to Joe. "I seriously don't know how he does it! That boy can sleep anywhere!"

Clearly not listening, Joe continues to stand rigidly with his back to me, staring into the tree line. I glance back at Will and notice that his face looks softer, even a little vulnerable as he sleeps. The smooth curves of his lips give the impression that he is smiling as he breathes slow, rhythmic breaths. A part of me is yearning to crawl in beside him, to rest my head in the hollow of his broad muscular shoulder, to share in his warmth and to lose myself in a dreamless sleep.

Tommy's yawning voice suddenly breaks my reverie.

"Don't know about you, Ally, but that's the best sleep I've had in ages."

I nod my head. "I guess Joe was right. Never thought that I could sleep out here… It must have been Mum. She helped us sleep."

Tommy smiles a sad smile. Unable to make eye contact, he walks over and joins Joe at the edge of the rock. Mimicking Joe's stance, Tommy folds his arms across his chest and stares out into the darkness too.

Taking the opportunity to have a quiet moment, I rifle through my rucksack to look at my provisions. I have never been much of a girlie girl, but as I rummage through my bag, I realise I have no brush, no toothbrush, essentially nothing that would make me feel a little more human right now. Life on the run officially sucks. Why is it that when you know that you can't brush your teeth, your mouth feels the furriest it's ever felt? Feeling hopeful, I realise there is a small chance that Joe may have something in his rucksack – the one that Will is currently sleeping on. To make do, I grab the water canister and take a mouthful, swishing the cool water around my mouth and quickly spitting it out onto the ground.

Joining the others at the edge of the rock, I whisper to Joe, "So… no Infected yet?"

He shakes his head. "No, nothing. Dunno if the girl has anything to do with it. I heard some far away in the distance, but nothing we need to worry about right now."

Tommy suddenly wrinkles his nose next to me and then dramatically cups his hands over his face, almost as though he is shielding himself from some mystery smell. Taking a step away from him, I suddenly feel paranoid that it's me. I quickly turn around to do a breath test into my own hands, feeling a little embarrassed.

With a look of sheer disgust on his face, Tommy looks at Joe and me accusingly.

"What is that smell? Did someone fart or something? If evil had a smell, it would smell like that!"

I furrow my brow and sniff the air around us to understand what Tommy is referring to. Joe initially looks confused but then a flash of realisation quickly spreads across face.

"Infected…"

Joe and I instantly draw our swords and begin to scramble down the boulders. Tommy jumps forward and grabs the hood of my jacket.

"Hang on. I can't hear anything!"

I almost trip over my own feet. "What do you mean you can't hear anything?"

Tommy searches the tree line.

"If they were that close, surely I would hear them, right? I heard Joe coming before he got here, and I can't hear anything other than wildlife and… Will's breathing!"

Cursing under his breath, Joe marches up to the top again, completely frustrated.

"I know you're trying to help here, kid, but we don't know how these abilities work yet. I heard some Infected a while ago, so Alyx and I need to run the perimeter to make sure."

Ignoring the sense of dread rising through me, I swallow hard and stare at them with an air of defiance.

"He was right about you, Joe. We could use this to our advantage. I think we should trust his instincts."

Tommy smiles at me meekly, almost grateful for my undying faith in him. In response, he points his face into the gentle breeze and closes his eyes. Nodding his head at us, he says, "The smell comes and goes in the wind, so they are probably quite far away. Sorry, false alarm."

Joe frowns as his mind races; trusting Tommy's abilities essentially goes against his military instincts.

"Okay, I'm not sure how happy I am about this… but given how dark it is, I guess we can wait it out and hope for the best."

Sighing heavily, his shoulders sag with exhaustion. Hesitating at first, he reluctantly places his sword back into its sheath and shakes his head with dismay.

"Between Tommy's abilities, the wild girl and the Infected, I'm fresh outta ideas!"

Tommy turns away from us, looking a little hurt by Joe's bluntness. Clearly unaware of his feelings, or maybe just too tired to notice, Joe slumps down on the edge of the rock and hangs his legs off the side. I reach out and reassuringly place my hand on Tommy's shoulder, acknowledging him, before joining Joe on the ground. I follow his gaze and squint into the darkness.

Without looking at me he mumbles, "You know that

Will should go back to Merope, kid? He should never have come out here in the first place. We clearly have so much more than just the Infected to worry about. He has his own family to think about."

My stomach lurches at the thought of Will leaving us. With a fluttering nervous feeling in my chest, the words suddenly explode from my mouth: "You can't send him back!"

Joe shushes at me. "Keep your voice down. I know we needed him, and without him we may never have escaped, but what about his family back in Merope? This is our battle, our problem, not Will's."

I hiss through gritted teeth, "If Will goes, I go. I'm not going anywhere without him, and you said yourself that they would kill us all on sight, so surely that includes Will?"

I continue to stare at him with my heart in my throat.

"He can't leave."

Not backing down, Joe turns away from me.

"I'll discuss it with Will when he wakes up."

Feeling as though I have had the air sucked out of my lungs, I angrily jump to my feet and walk as far away from Joe as possible. There's no point discussing this any further until Will is awake and at my side, especially with the kind of mood that Joe is in. He may be right, Will does have his own family, but I know in my heart that he would never leave us out here. With the night's chill starting to creep into my bones, I sulkily pull my hood up around my face again and shuffle back slightly so that my hips are next to Will's.

As I stare at his messy hair and angular jaw, something deep inside is drawing me in like a magnet. Unable to help myself, I angle my body towards his and slowly reach out, delicately brushing my fingers against the back of his hand. Still fast asleep, out of nowhere, he gently intertwines his warm, calloused fingers with mine. At his touch, I gasp as a tiny electrical pulse flows through my body, instantly making me shiver. He exhales quietly as a contented smile spreads from the corner of his soft mouth. Warmness spreads through my chest as I silently realise something I already knew; despite what Joe thinks, Will isn't leaving any time soon.

The sun has started to paint the morning sky red as it rises behind the shadowed trees. Amazingly Will managed to sleep all the way through to dawn without any interruptions from teenage assassins or the Infected. Gently waking him up, I lean over, placing my hand on his shoulder.

"Time to get up."

With his eyes still shut he groans, "Only if you have a sausage sandwich for me, then I might consider it…"

Just as I'm about to roll my eyes at him, an undead shriek echoes through the forest, and from the sound of it, it wasn't far away. I grin at him as I continue to lean over.

"Well, I can't offer you a sausage sandwich, but I can offer you the opportunity to hunt some Infected and maybe a dry biscuit?"

He opens his green eyes now.

"There's nothing quite like decapitating the dead and a dry biscuit to get you started!"

Beaming, I present my hand to him, offering to help him to his feet. Catching me off guard, he grabs my hand, yanking it hard towards him. Now completely off balance, I ungraciously fall on top of him against his hard, muscular chest. As our bodies collide, blood rushes to my cheeks, making them rosy red and flushed. He laughs heartily, clearly not sharing my awkwardness.

Joe quickly stomps over and yanks his rucksack out from underneath us.

"Stop fooling around. There's Infected out there, and we gotta make some serious ground today."

Feeling even more self-conscious, I quickly jump to my feet while trying to hide my annoyingly red cheeks with a curtain of hair. Tommy looks at me out of the corner of his eye, judgementally noting my embarrassment before heading to the bottom.

Ignoring them both, I grab my rucksack and stride to the edge of the boulders with my head held high. Will quickens his pace to join me, looking far too smug for my liking. Feeling a little less flushed, I continue to race ahead without looking at him.

"You know you're a jerk, right?"

Will pulls a pretend shocked face. "Can't believe you would say such a thing. Not my fault you're too weak to pull up my awesome body!"

At that, I quickly dig him in the ribs. "Thanks, you have just affirmed my previous statement… you're a jerk!"

Striding ahead purposefully, I reach the bottom and draw my sword, readying myself for the incoming Infected. Tommy stands nervously by the edge of the tree line waiting for me.

"I don't have a weapon, and Joe won't give me a gun."

I automatically kneel on the ground, grab my trusty dagger from inside my boot and hold it out for him. As he reaches out to take it from me I warn, "This dagger used to belong to Dad and is for emergency use only. You stay close and act as my wingman, pointing out where they are, got it?"

He nods his head with wide eyes. "Will there really be that many?"

I shrug my shoulders. "Don't know. Guess we will find out in a minute. Just stay out of trouble."

"I'll try…" he replies, smiling nervously.

Grabbing his shoulder, I gently push him forward and start jogging into the forest. Up ahead, Will and Joe have slowed their pace and carefully step over the razor wire. With their swords drawn, they creep through the underbrush, trying to make as little noise as possible. Tommy nervously paces in front, constantly looking over his shoulder at me. I glare at him and point ahead, reminding him to concentrate on where he is walking. I slow my breathing and focus all my senses on my surroundings, desperately trying to ignore the deafening sound of my heartbeat pounding in my ears.

My skin prickles as several undead moans echo through the trees; ahead Joe and Will instantly halt in response. Will's face drains of colour as a look of sheer horror spreads across it.

Upping my pace, I join them and witness the reason for their panic; struggling through the trees is a horde of over twenty Infected. Swallowing back bile, my legs start to feel weak. I have never fought this many at one time before.

Joe whispers hurriedly, "You know what to do. Just as I taught you. We can do this!"

I nod my head furiously.

He continues, "Everyone protect Tommy. Swords first and then guns if we become overwhelmed."

Will's jaw clenches as he grips his sword tightly. Joe raises his weapon and starts forward.

I pull Tommy in close and whisper, "Stay here at my side. If they get too close, use your dagger and aim for the head, got it?"

Looking like a frightened rabbit, he stares at me and bites his bottom lip. Not waiting for his response, I slowly step forward with adrenaline burning through my veins. At the sight of us, a deep resonant growl ripples through the group like a deafening tidal wave. Many of them missing arms and legs drag their rancid, decomposed bodies through the forest, whereas the more able-bodied Infected almost start running towards us.

To my right, Will stands poised and tensed, but his usual boyish charm is nowhere to be seen. He turns to me, emanating a mixture of determination and fear.

"I would never have left you."

My breath catches in my throat as I stare into his intense green eyes. Before I can respond, he suddenly runs head-on into the horde without looking back.

WINTER IN THE SPRING

In one elegant swoop, Will decapitates two Infected at the front of the horde. He quickly pushes the headless bodies into the oncoming crowd, sending several Infected stumbling backwards. Joe spears another through the mouth and slices through the top of its head. He quickly shoves the lifeless body to one side and instantly pushes ahead with Will flanked at his side.

Widening my stance, I meet my first Infected. Grabbing it by the neck forcefully, I thrust my sword upwards through its head and pull it away with ease. Without a moment's rest, another one staggers out from behind a tree, but none of my previous training could have prepared me for this. At the sight of her, a gasp escapes from my lips, making my grip weaken on my sword.

A little girl probably no older than six years old sways next to the tree. She's wearing a blood-stained nightgown with the remains of a comfort blanket dangling from her tiny hand. Her long, matted hair hangs limply, partially masking the black veins scattered on her snarling face. At the sight of me, a growl rumbles deep inside her chest as the blanket drops to the forest floor. With her arms outstretched, she takes a step forwards, revealing a nasty bite wound on her wrist.

As she approaches, my eyes slowly fill with tears, instantly blurring my vision. Taking in a shuddery breath, I shakily raise my sword as the little girl closes the distance between us. In that moment of pure vulnerability, I feel as though I have been hit by a train. A sharp pain radiates in my side, knocking the breath out of my lungs. My head begins to swim when I realise that I am actually falling. My sword flies out of my grasp and clangs to the floor out of reach, as the forest begins to spin uncontrollably. As I struggle to breathe, an Infected man the size of a grizzly bear pins me to the ground, crushing me underneath.

My hand shoots out in front of me and grabs the thing by the throat as I attempt to reach for my sword. Pushing with all my strength, the gigantic man dribbles black putrid goo all over my chest. Gritting my teeth, I cry out as its gnashing mouth edges closer and closer to my exposed neck. The little girl is now at my feet and begins to grab at my boots. I kick out furiously in response as tears continue to streak down my face.

Adjusting my grip, I quickly fumble for the gun tucked in my belt loop as the man inches closer to my jugular. Gripping it tightly, I press the muzzle of the gun underneath his chin and scream out in one last show of strength. I pull the trigger, and his head whips backwards, showering me in blood and gore. The man slumps on top of me, trapping me underneath; the stench is almost too much to bear as I try to roll the thing off me.

Struggling for breath, I lie on my back gasping for air, and my ears ring from the deafening sound of the gunshot. My side throbs in pain as a feeling of nausea thickens my throat. What if I've been bitten? Taking a deep breath, I quickly lift up my shirt to reveal a purplish bruise spreading across my ribs; I have never been so pleased to crack a rib in my life.

As I try to steady myself and take in my surroundings, I finally notice that the little girl is lying face down on the forest floor with my dagger nestled in the back of her head. Tommy stares at me in complete shock with tears streaming down his face.

Swallowing back my own horror, I crawl forward and rigidly retrieve the dagger, desperately resisting the urge to vomit. I hold the dagger out for him once more, and he stares at it momentarily, before shaking his head and refusing to take it from me.

Barely above a whisper I plead, "You did what you had to do."

As I climb to my feet, I see a flash of something white rushing through the trees just as more Infected round the corner. Will races through the crowd, coming to my aid. He's covered in congealed blood and chunks of flesh.

As he runs, he decapitates two Infected as they attempt to stagger towards me. Tommy stands beside me in an almost catatonic state, clearly still in shock. Before Will arrives, I despatch the last of the Infected in my vicinity and lean heavily against a tree, feeling weary. Will looks at us, concerned.

"You okay, Ally?"

Before I can respond, a noise reverberates through the trees, almost as loud as a thunder crack. Will and I stare upwards, searching the clear sky for the source of the sound. Completely confused, we quickly realise that whatever it was, it wasn't thunder. Behind me, I hear Tommy struggling. We spin around to find him pinned by an Infected.

Cursing myself for not paying attention, I run straight for him with my sword held high. Tommy suddenly launches the Infected into the air and throws it like a rag doll. It cracks its head against a tree and slumps to the ground.

Stunned, I stand rooted to the spot. My nervous teenage brother has morphed into some kind of killing machine. Tommy glares back at me with clenched fists, breathing heavily. The grief-stricken boy that just ended the little girl is nowhere to be seen. His eyes suddenly dart to my feet, as an Infected with no legs grabs at my boots. At lightning speed, he dashes forward and stamps on it as he runs into the remaining crowd. I turn to see Will standing there slack-jawed, probably mirroring my own expression.

An Infected seizes the opportunity and catches Will off guard by grabbing for his face. In shock, he stumbles backwards as it falls on top of him. I cry out and lunge for the monster pinning Will to the ground.

Grabbing it by the shoulders, I pull with all my strength, giving Will enough room to end its miserable life. Using the length of his sword, he presses upwards sharply as it slumps forwards onto his chest. In disgust, he pushes the thing off him and rolls to his feet.

As the crowd finally thins, I see Joe finishing off the last of them, but Tommy is nowhere to be seen. Fear begins to rise in my chest as I blindly stumble forwards, desperately trying not to slip on the river of body parts now strewn across the floor. Panic surges through me as I call out for Tommy, feeling terrified that I have failed to protect him once more.

I'm filled with momentary relief when he finally responds, but his voice is guarded, and he is hidden behind a large oak tree. Rushing to his side, I skid around the corner to discover that Tommy isn't alone; standing a few paces in front of him is the wild girl with long, wavy white hair.

Without moving a muscle, her intense electric-blue eyes look past Tommy and bore into mine. The hem of her moss-green dress flaps in the breeze as she continues to stare at me, poised like a cobra.

Will steadily steps out from behind a tree and faithfully joins my side. At the sight of him, her hand jerks, making the thick black whip cascading from her hand twitch. That must be the source of the sound that we heard earlier. Joe casually paces towards her, wipes the blood from his sword absentmindedly.

"What's your name, kid?"

Her eyes dart to Joe's mouth, but the girl remains silent. Pursing her lips into a hard line, she remains mute and continues to stare at Joe. Furrowing his brow, he swallows his impatience.

"You do understand the question?"

She stares at his mouth again as a smile creeps across her face. Joe tenses reflexively as she starts to bring her free hand up to her face. Not taking any chances, and with Tommy far too close, I grab the gun tucked into my belt loop and aim it directly at her forehead.

"Don't move, just answer the question."

Tilting her head slightly, the whip in her hands suddenly glows neon blue as a smirk quivers at the corner of her mouth. She starts to raise her hand once more but much quicker this time. Clicking the safety off, I grit my teeth.

"I mean it. Don't move!"

She holds her hand up next to her face and points to her ear. Joe exhales loudly beside me and shakes his head.

"She's deaf, kid."

Without taking my eyes off her, I respond cautiously. "How do we know she's not lying?"

Joe holds up his free hand and points to his mouth as he speaks, "You read lips?"

Her eyes dart to his mouth once more, and with an almost smug expression she nods her head steadily. Joe begins to calculate his next move.

"Okay, kid, drop the weapon and we can talk." The girl narrows her eyes at him as he continues, "Alyx, drop the gun."

"Not with Tommy that close to her."

Trying to diffuse the situation, he holds up his hands. "Okay, Tommy, nice and easy. Start making your way back to us."

Tommy slowly steps backwards, and as a show of good faith, Joe drops his sword to his feet and kicks it towards her, quickly followed by Will. Joe then gestures to her, trying to encourage the wild girl to do the same. The girl glares at me, silently demanding that I lower my gun first. With my jaw set firmly, I reluctantly ram the thing back into my belt loop as she lets her whip fall to the ground with snakelike grace. Joe takes a few guarded steps forwards.

"We ain't here to start anything, kid, so let's just start with your name."

Mimicking Joe, she holds her hands up and points to a satchel bag hanging at her waist.

Joe nods his head at her.

"If you need something from your bag to communicate, we gotta search it first, sweetheart."

Moving her weight to her other leg impatiently, the girl swiftly chucks her bag at my feet. Trying to ignore her glare, I scoop it off the ground and quickly search through it: a knife, rope, change of clothes and what looks like a piece of black slate. I hold the slate up for her to see. She nods her head and sarcastically mimes at me for something to write with. I reach to the bottom of her bag and find a dusty piece of chalk jammed in the corner. With the chalk and slate in hand, I carefully make my way over to her. As soon as I present it to her, she suddenly snatches it from my grasp.

Feeling irritated by her attitude, I snap, "If you keep this up, I'll tie you to this tree and leave you for the Infected!"

She smirks and laughs silently, which only makes me want to smash her in the face even more. Trying to take the high ground and keep my temper in check, I take a deep breath and slowly walk backwards to join the others.

She stares at us curiously as she idly twiddles the chalk between her fingers, almost as though she is assessing our worth. From the glint in her eye it's clear that whoever this girl is, she is fearless and will do whatever it takes to survive.

With his patience waning, an agitated Joe opens his mouth to challenge her, but before he utters a single word, she quickly scribbles something on the slate. She studies it and tilts her head to one side before slowly turning it over for us to see; in spidery letters filling the entire slate is the word *Winter*.

GOING COMMANDO

Winter quickly scrubs away her name with her wrist and slams the slate back into her bag. She purposefully points to each of us and demands that we give her our names. Her electric-blue eyes focus on me as she slowly folds her arms across her chest. Joe enunciates as he speaks, pointing to each of us in turn. Tilting her head to one side, she arches her eyebrow at Joe, prompting him to reveal his plan.

"Okay, kid, now we are acquainted we can get right into it. Thank you for your help back there. We all appreciate it. Out here you gotta be cautious, and I'm sure you know all about that."

She nods her head once in response.

Joe points to her whip. "I'm not even going to ask how you got your hands on one of those. That's a military-grade weapon that is only issued to the most skilled fighters. In fact, I've never actually seen one in the flesh, only ever heard about it because of its reputation."

A smirk twitches at the corner of her mouth as he continues, "I don't see any other folks with you, so I assume you're out here by yourself?"

As I stare at her, I glimpse a flicker of pain in her eyes; she purses her lips tightly as she nods once more. Joe, noting it too, lowers his head slightly before continuing.

"Well, kid, we could do with your help. Can you show us to the next walled town?"

She stares back at him, clearly suspicious.

"We don't have a lot, but I'll make it a worthy trade. That's a promise."

Joe and Winter exchange a knowing look as she calculates his offer; with a curt nod she quickly bends down and grabs her whip from the ground. At her touch, it suddenly glows neon blue, and the light almost throbs between her fingers. Not wasting any time, she turns on her heel and trudges into the thick forest, pushing branches from her path as she goes.

Will slowly bends down to grab his sword from the ground and is clearly on edge by the trade-off. He grits his teeth as he starts forward.

"Dunno what the hell that was about, but I guess she's agreed to show us then, huh?"

I wipe my sword of Infected gore and ask, "Are you sure about this, Joe? I don't trust her at all!"

He exhales loudly. "No, but one thing I know is that I am smarter, older and more experienced. Besides, if she was going to kill us all, she would have tried it already."

I quickly study my sword before I place it back into its sheath. I look to Tommy who is standing poised and focused. His fists are clenched so tightly that his veins are popping in his forearm. My stomach flips and my palms become sweaty; I can't help but fear what has become of my little brother. I sling my rucksack onto my shoulder and push away an errant hair that is plastered to my face with sweat and grime. Tommy follows Will, leaving me and Joe behind.

As we start forward, Joe murmurs under his breath, "Everything is going to be okay…"

At first I think he is trying to reassure me, but after studying his expression, I realise that he may be trying to reassure himself. Filled with dread, I hold my head high and lightly place my hand on the hilt of my sword, following Winter into the unknown.

We march on in silence; the tension is palpable as Winter continues to hike upfront at an unrelenting pace. As I try to keep up, the balls of my feet begin to throb, and my arms are shredded by the thickets of the trees. Fortunately, I don't seem to have any blisters yet. From the position of the sun, I can tell we've been walking for hours with no signs of a walled village, or any Infected for that matter. But the further we go, the more I begin to panic. Beside me, Joe paces steadily with a solemn expression.

Not wanting to draw any attention, I whisper to him, "Any idea where we are?"

Quickly searching his surroundings, he says, "I have a vague idea. After I rescued you and your brother, I knew I had to take you somewhere safe. I heard that there were two walled villages in this part of the country, and Merope was the first one I came across… but I have no idea what this other place is like."

Up ahead, Will slows down to join me and Joe. "What's the deal, Joe? We seem to be following this white-haired assassin into the abyss all for a vague trade-off. What's the angle here?"

Patting him on the back, Joe replies, "Don't worry, kid. It's all in hand."

Joe pushes forward, leaving me and Will at the

back. With a worried expression, Will turns to me. "Not sure if I like this, Ally."

"Me either, but one thing I do know is I trust Joe with my life, so I'm sure he knows what he's doing."

Nodding his head, his expression softens. "Yeah, I hope so. Oh, and by the way, I meant what I said. I would never have left you if Joe had asked me to."

Blood threatens to rush to my cheeks, but I ignore it and try to sound nonchalant. "Well, I suppose you're okay to have around sometimes."

Will puts his arm around my shoulders. "Well, I know your life would be dull without me, so I can't really blame you for not wanting me to leave."

Shaking my head, I say, "You're such a douche, in fact, maybe I've just changed my mind!"

"Well, let's be honest, Ally," Will says with a sad smile, "My mum probably hasn't even noticed that I've been gone for two days anyway."

Will's mum likes a drink, and when I say a drink, I mean a lot of very alcoholic drinks; some folks haven't taken too well to the apocalypse in one way or another. Who can blame them? The loss of family and friends, the constant threat of infection, living in a walled community on rations – they say the ones that survive in this new world are the ones that had it tough before the old world ended. Survivors always find a way to keep on surviving; it's in their blood. At the thought of his mum, the momentary relief from our banter has quickly vanished. Ahead Winter slows down to a normal pace, and I can hear the faint sound of water flowing through the forest. We must be approaching the river again.

As the trees begin to thin, Winter stands near the banks

of the river and waits for us to join her; she points to the other side, implying that we need to cross over. Joe takes a few steps forward to assess the situation. The river isn't fast moving, which is probably why she has chosen this point to cross; however, it does look deep, which means that we will probably need to swim.

The clear blue water flows lazily downstream, and the sun bounces off the surface, making the river sparkle like diamonds in the sunlight. Considering that we are all covered in blood and guts from this morning, I have never been more relieved to have a wash.

Winter shoves her whip into her satchel and begins to strip off her clothes, revealing her small, athletic frame. Joe quickly averts his eyes, clearly more embarrassed than she is. Will, on the other hand, continues to gawp at her open-mouthed.

She flicks her long, wavy white hair behind her, letting it cascade down the centre of her back. She starts to pace towards the water and stuffs her dress and boots into her satchel before pausing momentarily to unhook her bra. At this point, Will finally averts his eyes and even blushes a little in response.

As I stare at Will incredulously, a pang of jealousy radiates in my chest, making my heart sink into my stomach. Winter wades into the water with her bag held over her head; she then launches her satchel to the river bank on the other side and then dives under the surface like a mermaid. Joe clears his throat, breaking the silence between all of us.

"Okay, kids, guess we can take this opportunity to get cleaned up. I have some soap in my kit, so we can all take turns."

Joe steps towards Tommy, who has remained silent and surly. He reaches out to place his hand on his shoulder, but Tommy flinches from his touch.

"Come on, kid. Why don't you get yourself cleaned up?"

Tommy grits his teeth and glares at Joe. From his expression, he looks as though he may lash out at any moment. Joe opens his mouth to try and dissipate the situation, but Tommy angrily starts to remove his clothes and leaves them in a pile on the ground. He dashes forwards and dives into the water.

Winter resurfaces following all the commotion. Still partially submerged under the water, she narrows her electric-blue eyes and regards him curiously before disappearing once more. Joe exhales loudly, looking weary. He riffles through his rucksack, reaching for the soap. Holding his hand out, he offers it to me first, but I shake my head in response.

"It's fine. You go first."

Forcing a smile, he collects Tommy's clothes from the ground before pacing to the edge of the water, leaving me and Will alone. I stare down at my feet not wanting to make eye contact with Will, partly because I'm feeling a little pouty that he clearly checked out Winter and partly because I need to strip down to my underwear in front of him.

Will shrugs beside me and unbuttons his hoody. He casually takes off his T-shirt, revealing his perfectly toned torso; he absentmindedly fiddles with his belt buckle and slips his khakis down to his ankles. He looks at me with a coy expression without uttering a single word.

Taking a deep breath, I realise that it's now or never. At lightning speed, I whip off my t-shirt, clearly forgetting about my bruised ribs. Wincing in pain, I suck in a sharp breath through my teeth and slowly bend round to have a look at the damage. Will is instantly at my side and reaches out, gently hovering his hand over the bruise.

"Are you okay, Ally? Do you need me?"

I look up to see Will staring down at me with eyes full of concern, wearing nothing but his underwear. I bite my bottom lip when I realise that there are only inches between us. Joe whistles from the water, instantly breaking the tension between us. He glares at Will, giving him a warning look; the one that only a father can give to the boyfriend of his teenage daughter. Will swallows and then clears his throat awkwardly.

Feeling a little breathless I murmur, "I'm okay..."

Will smiles at me crookedly and then paces into the river, leaving me behind. Feeling a little flushed, I pull down my own khakis and kick off my boots, shoving them straight into my rucksack. With my sword in one hand and my rucksack in the other, I walk barefoot towards the water's edge in my underwear. I pause momentarily and briefly consider removing my bra like Winter and then quickly dismiss the idea. Even though I only have one bra, I would rather hike in wet underwear than swim around topless like Winter.

I dip my toes into the freezing cold water and gasp as the water splashes up my legs. I launch my bag to the other side of the river and wade in deeper, holding my sword over my head.

Joe swims towards Will and me, takes our weapons and then passes the soap.

"You kids have five minutes."

Feeling a little self-conscious, I lather the soap in my

hands and scrub my face until it's pink and tingly; then I wash my hair twice and desperately try to detangle it with my fingers as I go. This army-issue soap is probably going to wreck my hair. I finally swim over to Will, who has been floating around on his back basking in the sun, waiting for me to finish. He grins at me and holds his hand out.

"Ah, looking decidedly more human now, Ally!"

I give him a withering look and slap the soap into his hand before swimming ashore. As I near the shallows, Joe and Tommy are standing awkwardly to one side with some distance between them. Winter, on the other hand, is crouched on the floor and focused on scribbling something on her slate.

I meekly grab my own rucksack and then grab Joe's rucksack before disappearing behind a tree to get dressed. By the time I return, Will is standing on the riverbank in his underwear, dripping wet. His eyes dazzle as he grabs his bag and starts to get dressed in front of us. Winter stands up abruptly and passes her slate to Joe.

Furrowing his brow, he tries to decipher the messy writing before he says, "The walled village is up ahead, kids."

Winter points ahead of her, affirming the direction. Joe then passes the slate back to her before he continues, "A deal's a deal, Winter. I promised that I would make it worth your while…"

Joe draws his sword and studies it lovingly, turning it over from side to side almost as though he is memorising its beauty. Sighing with nostalgia, he holds out his beloved sword and presents it to Winter. I can't help but gasp in surprise. Joe turns and glares at me, warning me to keep my mouth shut.

He continues, "After my family, this is my most valued item in my life. I trust this has made the journey worthwhile?"

Without hesitating she steps forward and takes the sword from his grasp; she smiles as she feels the weight of it in her tiny hands. Taking a few steps back, she lightly spins on the spot, testing the sword's worthiness with cat-like grace. Her long, ice-white hair flows behind her, as she slices the sword through a tree branch beside her.

Stopping suddenly, her eyes glisten as she purposefully paces towards an unarmed Joe. Will steps to his side instinctively and grabs his sword in defence. Ignoring Will, she stands poised with a solid stance, still clutching the sword tightly. Her electric-blue eyes focus on Joe as she suddenly closes the distance between them; a smile quivers at the corner of her mouth, as she unexpectedly presents her free hand to Joe. Nodding his head in approval he shakes her hand firmly.

"Thank you, Winter."

Her eyes glisten as she quickly turns on her heel, heading into the trees. Before she disappears, she pauses momentarily and unzips a small hidden pocket on the front of her satchel. She studies the object in her hand with a mischievous smile etched onto her face. She quickly spins around and gently throws it to Joe, who catches it in one hand reflexively.

He opens his hand as we all crowd around to study the object: it's a tiny carved wooden figurine of a man with a sword held firmly at his side. A smile begins to form at the corner of Joe's mouth. We all look up and realise that Winter has suddenly vanished.

Joe raises his eyebrows as he mutters, "Well I'll be damned…"

THE BIGGER PICTURE

Joe chuckles to himself as he turns the figurine over and over between his fingers. Will and I, on the other hand, stare at him dumbfounded by his decision to trade his beloved sword. Joe's sword is truly one of a kind; the dark leather binding wrapped around the hilt of the sword is carved with intricate patterns that Joe painstakingly crafted himself.

When we first arrived at Merope, every night he would put me and Tommy in bed and then stay up into the early hours of the morning tapping away, carving the most beautifully detailed floral tribute. Once he had finished, he got blind drunk and admitted that each of the flower buds were in remembrance of the friends that he lost in his platoon during the first wave of infection, and the two large roses intertwined at the top of the hilt were for his brother-in-law and his sister: my mum and dad.

At the time, I was too young to appreciate or even understand how awful that time must have been for Joe, and clearly carving this leather was an outlet for his grief. During the first few weeks in Merope, whenever I felt sad about my mum and dad, Joe would point at the roses on his sword and remind us that they would always be with us, fighting the war against the infection.

A lump begins to rise in my throat as I shake my head in disbelief. Feeling lost for words I mumble, "How could you, Joe? Your sword…"

Looking miserable, he holds up his hand to stifle me.

"It's a small sacrifice to pay for the bigger picture. If she hadn't helped us, we could have been wandering around for days in search of this damn place. The quicker we get our provisions and get to Alhena, the quicker we can get help for Tommy." He presses his lips into a hard line and stares at me defiantly. "It was the right thing to do."

Tommy crosses his arms over his chest at the mention of his name, and for the first time since the battle this morning, he looks almost remorseful. Joe notices the small change in Tommy's body language and clears his throat.

"Anyway, it's done now, so there's no use mourning over it. Let's try and get into this damn village."

I chew my bottom lip. "Try and get into…?"

"Some places don't take too kindly to outsiders. No doubt they will want to search us for bites and question us on our intentions; pretty standard procedure for folks showing up unannounced."

My heart sinks at the thought of another night out here exposed to the elements and the Infected. I hope they let us in. Tommy stands behind Will, fidgeting with wide eyes. Exhaling, he starts to jog in the direction of the village.

Darting forward, Joe grabs Tommy's shirt and hisses, "Easy there, kid. We have to approach with caution, which means you guys stay here while I go and talk to them. Besides, we could all do with some food and water before we go in. We are gonna need to be at full strength today."

Sulking, Tommy joins us once more and slumps down

onto the ground, leaning heavily against the base of a tree. Joe riffles through the rucksack and starts pulling out food and throwing it to Will and me. He crouches down and hesitates before passing an apple to Tommy.

"Let's not have a repeat of last time. If you start gnawing on this like an animal, it's the only thing you're eating, got it?"

Looking a little embarrassed, he takes the apple meekly, but his pupils dilate at the sight of food. Visibly straining, he slowly takes a bite from the apple, resisting the urge to scoff the whole thing in two seconds flat.

Joe watches him like a hawk as a bead of sweat forms on Tommy's brow. Once Tommy is finished, Joe is clearly satisfied with his level of restraint and passes him the last of the sweet biscuits before we all pack up to leave.

As we gather our weapons, I hold out my hand and pass my dagger to Joe; he hesitates before slowly taking it from my grasp. With sad eyes, he gently studies it, feeling the weight of it in his hand before giving me a curt nod and placing it in his belt loop. As I sling the rucksack on my shoulder, Joe checks the shells in his shotgun before trudging in the direction of the village with Tommy at his side. Will waits for me and walks in step.

"Are you ready for this, Ally?"

"Guess I don't have a choice but to be ready."

Smiling at me with a cheeky grin, he says, "Come on, Ally, what's the worst thing that could happen?"

My heart flutters in my chest as I ponder Will's words. After everything that has happened to us, how could it possibly get any worse?

Joe slowly pushes his way through the thick understorey

between the trees, as we stealthily approach the clearing. Before he walks out into the open, he pulls us all in for a huddle and whispers, "Okay, so I'm going in first. I want you all to stay here on high alert, keeping your wits about you. If all goes to plan, I will whistle for you to join me. If it all goes… horribly wrong, then, Alyx, you'll be in charge. Head for Alhena and don't look back."

Joe stares at me decisively and places his hand firmly on my shoulder.

"All you'll need to do is find Mia Rose. We were in the same battalion in the army. She will help you."

I nod my head furiously but my hands begin to shake at the prospect of it all going 'horribly wrong'. Joe slaps me on the back and smiles at me, trying to reassure us. With twinkling eyes, he looks at me earnestly.

"Don't worry, kiddo. I'll see you soon!"

Without waiting for a response, he heads through the trees into the open. Now out of view, I jump to my feet and draw my sword, feeling overwhelmingly agitated. Will begins to scan our surroundings for anyone potentially watching us, whereas I lean against a tree and focus my hearing on anything that could be happening to Joe.

Tommy's bizarre expression catches my attention; his wild eyes dart around him as he looks somewhere between angry and frightened. My heart sinks as I realise that getting into the walled village isn't our only challenge. We also need to try and hide Tommy's 'abilities' from the people of the town, and from looking at his demeanour, I wonder if that's even possible. I reach out to him to try and ease his tension.

I whisper, "Everything is going to be okay. I'm here with you. I won't let anything happen to you, I promise."

Cutting me off, he speaks for the first time since this morning.

"I'm fine. Just feeling… nervous."

Will and I share a troubled look. Tommy has been becoming more and more unpredictable since the incident with the little girl. I open my mouth to try and soothe Tommy further, but a deep voice resonates in the distance, breaking my attention.

"Sir, do not approach any further. We are armed and ready to shoot. Please drop your weapon immediately."

My heart races, and I feel as though it's going to burst out of my chest. Noticing my fear, Will steps towards me and places both hands on my shoulders.

"Don't do anything stupid, Ally. Joe knows what he's doing, and I think he already proved that with Winter."

I quickly nod at Will, but I'm so anxious that I can barely listen to him. I creep forward to the edge of the clearing and peep behind a tree. In the distance, I see the entrance of the village; the wooden gates tower over Joe as he stands with his hands held firmly behind his head. Although I can't hear what is being said or even see the people that he is talking to, I can see that he is speaking decisively.

Minutes feel like hours as they continue to talk inaudibly; adrenaline burns through me, making my anxiety even worse. Taking a step away, I rest my back against a tree, unable to take the tension anymore. As I close my eyes momentarily from exhaustion, the gates slowly begin to grind wide open. Will smiles at me lopsidedly.

"I believe that's our signal!"

Joe's whistle is like music to my ears. I exhale with relief and smile at Will. At least these people seem reasonable enough to let us stay for the night. Tommy jumps to his feet and starts running ahead, leaving me and Will for dust. Will points ahead to where Tommy is running towards Joe.

"How are we going to explain this one?"

I clutch my sword tightly, turning my knuckles white. Giving Will a blank expression, I confirm, "We're not."

Nodding his head, we start forward and approach the gates with caution. The village walls, unlike Merope, are solid stone at over a metre thick, not to mention they are topped with razor wire. This unyielding fortress looks more like a prison camp than a walled village. The stark contrast between the lush green forest and this gloomy grey metropolis is a sight to behold.

With the formidable walls towering at over twenty-five feet, I can't help but wonder, are they trying to keep out the Infected or are they trying to keep their people inside? I shield my eyes from the glaring sun to have a closer look and see soldiers standing to attention at intervals on the walls; each and every one of them has an array of military-grade weapons slung about their bodies.

Will tenses beside me as the soldiers gather at the top of the gates, anticipating our arrival. As we approach the opening, a river of putrid-smelling mud surrounds the entrance of the village, making me instantly wrinkle my nose in disgust. I quickly realise that there's no way to go around it. If we are going into this damn place then we are going to have to wade our way through that stuff. The combination of the towering walls, leering soldiers and rancid muck clinging to my boots, my stomach suddenly lurches in response.

I try to ignore the sense of dread gnawing deep inside

of me and push forward, but as soon as I round the corner I am suddenly confronted by another towering gate that has alarmingly remained closed. Joe eyes us steadily, desperately trying to reassure us, just as the soldiers overhead slowly shut the first gate behind us.

With a deafening creak, they secure the gate, essentially trapping us inside. My teeth chatter in my head as I begin to feel like a caged animal. In a blur, I holster my sword and whip out my pistol, wildly pointing the gun at the soldiers overhead. The men instantly pull out an array of guns, clicking off the safeties and aiming for our heads.

A voice screams, "Lower your gun!"

Joe is instantly at my side and hisses, "Ally, do as they say."

Frozen in fear, I continue to aim the pistol overhead as panic consumes me. An unseen soldier shouts, "Drop your weapon! This is your second warning!"

Will reaches out and places his warm hand in the small of my back, encouraging me to listen to Joe. Letting out a shaky breath, I steadily hold up my hands and drop the gun into the mud.

The voice continues, "Now put all your weapons on the floor, where we can see them."

Will exhales through gritted teeth as we both drop our beloved swords into the rancid mud. Tommy clenches his fists beside me, looking as though he may explode at any moment.

The unseen soldier continues, "Now sit tight. The general is on his way."

Joe speaks in a lowered voice, "They said that they can't let us in until he has seen us."

"The general?"

"Yeah, looks like he's in charge of this place. Given the calibre of the weapons these soldiers have and the level of security, I would say that this place is run by ex-military."

Will chimes in, "I hope so… otherwise what kind of person calls themselves the General?

Joe has a grim expression. "I guess we will find out soon enough."

The soldiers part overhead, making way for a formidable man at the top of the gate; all of them salute and stand to attention as they finally let him through. A greying older man, wearing an immaculate military uniform, with an angular hook nose and high cheekbones, rigidly leans forward. His soulless black eyes bore into Joe as he bares his yellowing teeth with disgust. Joe's face drains of colour and his eyes widen at the sight of him. I have never seen Joe look so horrified in my life. The general raises his chin as he finally acknowledges him.

"Lieutenant Joseph Hudson… we meet again."

WELCOME TO PANAMA

Joe remains silent as he sets his jaw firmly. The tension in the air is almost electrifying as the general continues to stare at Joe, waiting for a response. My thoughts cast back to Will's earlier comment on how things couldn't get any worse – apparently they can. The soldiers overhead remain poised and focused, staring at our every move. A handful of men have their weapons aimed at us, should we try something in the presence of the general. Exhaling slowly, Joe's shoulders remain tense as he finally acknowledges him in return.

"General Sinter."

Narrowing his eyes at Joe, he replies, "Welcome to Panama... I never thought that I would have the pleasure of your company again, after the day that you abandoned your brothers in the squad."

The general straightens his immaculate military uniform; he casually takes out a cigar from his pocket, chews off the end and then lights it before he continues, "You are a wanted man, Lieutenant. You're wanted as a deserter of the fight against the infection."

Joe stares at him and speaks through gritted teeth: "I had no choice but to leave. Do you think it was easy to do what I did?"

My pulse quickens as I whisper nervously at Joe, "What's he talking about?"

The general holds up his hand to stifle him and then continues to puff on his cigar. "Lieutenant Hudson swore his allegiance to protect this country, to rescue humanity from the brink of the apocalypse, to stand tall with his brothers shoulder to shoulder and fight against the Infected."

He pauses momentarily and glares at Joe, as a look of shame and anger crosses his face. "Lieutenant Hudson deserted his duty for you."

Joe straightens with an air of defiance.

"That's correct, sir. I chose to save the lives of my niece and nephew after my sister and brother-in-law were killed by the Infected. Alyx and Tommy would have died. They were only kids, Sinter."

With a blank expression, he stares at Joe with cold eyes. "How heroic of you, Lieutenant, but to be a soldier, you must make sacrifices, and that means making difficult choices. I am sure that I can speak for everyone here in this compound when I say that we have all made difficult choices at some point in our military careers."

I glance sideways and notice that Tommy is standing with his fists clenched, breathing erratically. If Tommy flips out now, they will kill us all. Joe tries to shrug off the general's spitefulness and stands tall.

"So, if you're supposedly still saving lives, why aren't you out there? Why are you holed up in this goddamned walled village? What did you call this place? Panama?"

The general glares in response. "It's called Panama, Lieutenant, because of the entrance into the compound. This gate system has become a highly efficient security measure for the wellbeing of all the occupants here in Panama. The compound had succumbed to the Infected much in the same way your sister's town did. We received a clean-up order and were told to reinforce the walls so that operations could commence once more."

Joe furrows his brow. "What operations?"

The general practically spits his response, "That's classified information, Lieutenant. Ironically, if you had continued your duty in the squad, then you would know the answer to that question." The general gestures behind himself. "But I'm sure that you are intelligent enough to deduce that this place has never been a civilian town, quite the contrary in fact."

He continues to stare at us as his eyes darken even more. "Now as you can imagine I am a busy man and don't like to waste my precious time on deserters, but before you can enter Panama, you're all going to have to remove your clothes. It's standard procedure for anyone that wishes to enter the compound."

Will steps forward and gestures down his body. "So, you want me to take my clothes off before you even buy me a drink? I have to say, I usually like to loosen up a little before I give up the goods…"

The general's face flushes bright red with anger, looking as though he may spontaneously combust. "You had better watch your mouth, son, otherwise I'll throw you out with no provisions, and I'll keep your weapons too. Maybe that will teach you some respect!"

Setting his jaw firmly, the general attempts to maintain composure.

"Given that you clearly have no supplies, otherwise you

would never have come here in the first place, you have two options: option number one is to take your clothes off so that we can do our jobs and then you can take full advantage of our facilities here, or option number two, I send my soldiers in, and they remove your clothes before sending you on your way. It's your call."

Will considers the choices. "How about option three? How about you let us all go, including Joe, and we can forget that this ever happened? You can go on back to whatever the hell it is you're doing here, and we can go on living our lives. I think that sounds pretty sweet, if you ask me."

Losing patience, the general leans forward. "Now I'm afraid that is impossible. Lieutenant Hudson must be punished for his crimes and face the consequences of his actions."

Joe looks to me with a pained expression but remains silent. The general raises his chin and speaks loudly and decisively to the soldiers surrounding him.

"Check them all for signs of infection, and throw Lieutenant Hudson in solitary. Make sure the others have enough supplies. They can stay if they wish, but if they even so much as put a finger out of line, send them on their way."

The general exits from the top of the gate just as quickly as he arrived, leaving his soldiers to do his bidding. At his command, four soldiers automatically drop off the edge of the wall with a thud, flicking putrid mud up our legs. As I look down at myself, I notice a rotten human ear next to my boot. Bile shoots into my throat as I nearly fall over trying to scramble away from it. Too horrified to speak, I point at the ear shakily while desperately trying to steady my breathing.

At the sight of it, Will approaches a huge soldier with a

shaved head. "Hey, muscles, there appears to be an ear in the mud. You might want to take a look at that?"

Ignoring him, he responds in a thick accent I can't place, "Remove your clothes, child."

With his cockiness subsiding, Will suddenly looks on edge. "Joe, I don't know who this general is, but I think we all need to get out of here right now."

Grinding his teeth, Joe stands rigidly. "I don't think it's an option for me to leave, kid, but once they have checked you all over, you need to get the hell out of here and get to Alhena."

I stand frozen to the spot still trying to process the fact that there's a human ear in the mud.

Noticing my expression, Joe swallows hard before speaking: "The squad dismembers and then burns the Infected."

Nauseated at the thought of standing in mulched-up Infected, my stomach finally empties its contents onto the ground. Feeling unsteady, I wipe the back of my hand against my lips and grimace as a residue of acrid bile coats the inside of my mouth. As I straighten, a soldier standing in front of me suddenly raises his weapon and presses the barrel of his assault rifle to my forehead. His dorky ears stick out from underneath his helmet as he glares at me leeringly. He smiles at me as we finally make eye contact.

"Time to get your kit off… It's been a while since I seen a pretty little thing like you."

Both Joe and Will take a step towards this guy, prompting the other soldiers to raise their guns. The dorky one continues, "Now, now, boys, no need to get yer panties in a twist. I promise I'll be nice and gentle…"

Joe's face flushes with anger. "Get the hell away from her!"

'Muscles' impatiently grabs at Will, encouraging him to start removing his clothes. Will dodges his grasp and then shoves the man back, squaring up to him.

"What the hell is your problem? I'm taking my damn clothes off!"

With my attention diverted, 'Dorky' closes the distance and places his hand on my hip. Without thinking, I punch him in the nose and take pleasure as blood explodes down his face.

Over the commotion Joe shouts, "That's enough, both of you!"

I whip my head round to find Joe and Tommy cornered by two men pointing their guns at their chests. Dorky spits at me indignantly and then snarls as he stares at me.

Joe holds his hands up and speaks firmly. "None of us are infected, okay? You can see for yourselves that we ain't. I'm asking you, man to man, please don't make Alyx take her clothes off here in front of him. Imagine if she was your daughter, sister, cousin, whatever… would you want that creep checking her over?"

Joe seems to have hit a raw nerve with the soldiers pinning him to the wall; their weapons begin to waver.

One murmurs to the other, "We could get Suzie to check her out?"

Dorky starts towards them. "Screw that, you heard the general. They gotta be strip-searched, and I ain't going to defy my orders like him."

The two soldiers standing in front of Joe nod their heads in agreement. "Sorry, mate, if the general finds out that we didn't search her, we will be done for."

Trying to comfort Joe, I hold my head up high.

"I'm fine, Joe, really. One of you guys can search me, but if this asshole even so much as glances in my direction, I'm going to cut something off him that will be missed!"

I wade my way towards Joe and the others, just as Will grins at Dorky and then winks at him as he approaches.

"Today is your lucky day! You get to check me over now, buddy, and man you're in for a treat!"

Dorky stares at Will, completely livid, which spurs Will on even more. "So how do we do this? Do you want me to do a little dance first or shall we just get straight down to it?"

I can't help but giggle, which angers Dorky even more. He raises the barrel of his gun and presses it to Will's forehead.

"Just get on with it!"

Shrugging his shoulders in response, Will starts to take his hoody off. "I guess I'll get straight to it then, huh?"

A woman in army fatigues leans over at the top of the wall; her round eyes, soft lips and blonde spiky hair contradicts her masculine uniform. She glares at the dorky soldier.

"Bobby, why does it not surprise me that you're perving all over some innocent girl? Just keep your dirty little paws…"

Suzie looks at a now topless Will, and he grins at her in response. "Don't worry. Alyx put him straight. Now he has the pleasure of checking me over instead!"

Rolling her eyes at him, Suzie drops off the edge of the wall and smiles at me sweetly. She briefly makes eye contact with Joe, looking momentarily shocked, and then quickly averts her gaze. As she approaches, she offers me a handshake.

"Hey, I'm Suzie. These jerks giving you a hard time?"

I shrug. "Nothing I can't handle."

"Good to hear. Now why don't we go over in the corner for a little privacy and get this over with, huh?"

Overwhelmingly relieved, I follow Suzie into the corner. She stands solidly in front of me, shielding me from any wandering eyes. Becoming inpatient, the other soldiers push for Joe and Tommy to quickly strip down to prove that they are not infected. The soldier examining Tommy flips him around and points his gun at his back.

"Hold up, son, what's this you got on your back?"

Tommy stiffens as the soldier leans in for a closer look.

Joe interjects quickly, "He got that from a fight with another kid at school. You can see he ain't infected."

Ignoring Joe, the soldier beckons one of his comrades to investigate as well. Whispering in hushed tones, they speak hurriedly and gesture towards Tommy's scratches. Wavering uncertainly, the first soldier nods his head firmly and confirms, "Okay, you're good to go, but I'm going to recommend that one of the doctors checks you out."

Feeling a little panicked, I try to remain calm. "Is that really necessary? He's clearly not infected."

Suzy stares at me earnestly. "It's just standard procedure. You can go with him if you would like? It's probably nothing, but we have to be extra cautious about everything and everyone that turns up here. I'm sure you understand."

Joe stares at me and nods his head, encouraging me not to push it any further. As I exhale I can't help but have a bad feeling about all of this. Suzie smiles at me, trying to reassure me, and then calls out to a soldier behind the closed gate.

"Okay, you can open up now!"

The gate begins to slowly grind open to reveal a team of soldiers waiting on the other side; one of them at the front is holding a pair of handcuffs and walks towards Joe. In an official tone he announces, "Lieutenant Joseph Hudson, I hereby arrest you on suspicion of desertion of your position in 52nd Infantry Division of Alhena. You don't have to say anything, but it may harm your defence if you do not mention, when questioned, something you later rely on during your trial. Anything you do say may be taken as evidence."

Joe holds his wrists out firmly in front of himself and stares at the man with a blank expression. With an air of defiance, he maintains eye contact as the man snaps the handcuffs tightly over his wrists. My breath catches in my throat as I stand by powerlessly as two heavily armed men grab at his arms forcibly and begin to drag him into the compound.

In a blur, Tommy attempts to run after the men detaining Joe, but Will anticipates his move and desperately tries to restrain him. Joe maintains eye contact and stares at me, filled with determination. He mouths the words 'trust Suzie' before he rounds a corner and disappears out of sight. My eyes begin to sting with tears as I turn to look at Suzie. With a grave expression, she almost anticipates my question.

"What are they going to do to him?"

Her skin pales as she takes in a shuddery breath.

"The punishment for desertion is death by firing squad."

HOME SWEET HOME

My legs begin to feel weak at the knees as black spots creep into the corner of my vision. Will is so preoccupied with Tommy that he clearly didn't hear Suzie. I place my hand on my forehead, trying to steady myself, as Suzie reaches out reflexively and puts her arm around my waist. She whispers hurriedly in my ear, but I can't focus on anything. All I can hear are the words 'death by firing squad' resonating over and over in my mind. My heart pounds as I finally make eye contact with Suzie.

With watery eyes, she stares at me earnestly and speaks in a lowered voice: "I know that we have only just met, but you need to come with me right now… I promise that you can trust me."

Anger bubbles inside my chest as I push her away from me. I know that Joe told me to trust this woman, but given she works for the same people that are going to try and kill him, it's not so damn easy. I hold up my hands and take a step back.

"Just give me a minute, okay? I need some room."

Tommy finally gives up trying to run off and stands there looking exhausted. Suzie mirrors my stance and holds her hands up too. With a measured voice, she nods her head before speaking.

"I know that you're feeling a little emotional right now, and you have every reason to doubt me, but considering your options, you don't have much choice. Please just come with me and hear me out."

Noting my expression, Will joins my side. "Everything okay?"

I look at Suzie and then Tommy. However angry I feel at these people right now, Tommy is better off not knowing the truth. In fact, it's better for all of us if Tommy doesn't know.

Trying to keep my voice even, I reply, "Everything is fine. Suzie has said that we can go with her, and she will help us."

Will eyes me suspiciously, clearly not believing me. I raise my chin and subtly point my head in the direction of Tommy.

He looks at Suzie and speaks with a gruff voice: "Thanks. We appreciate it."

Tommy's face flushes with anger as he throws his arms up in the air. "I'm not going anywhere without Joe!"

Trying to dissipate the situation, I step towards him and take his hands into mine.

"I don't want to either, but we need to sit down and think this through. If we go storming in without a plan and try to do something with all these soldiers everywhere, they will throw us out of here, and then we will all be screwed."

He stares at me with his light chocolate-brown eyes and furrows his brow with concern. I realise that he won't come quietly, so I need to pull at his heartstrings.

"I believed in you when no one else did. You could have

died back in Merope, and I was there for you. So, I need you to believe in me now, can you do that?"

Hesitating at first, he lowers his gaze, staring at his feet and then finally nods his head. Trying to remain calm, I turn to Suzie once more.

"Okay, fine, we'll go with you."

With a look of relief, she paces into the compound and gestures for us to follow her. Looking over her shoulder at us, she says, "Just keep your heads down, and don't wander off, okay?"

Will looks at me with eyes full of concern, but I shake my head in response, silently informing him to leave it alone. As I stare down the alley where the soldiers dragged Joe, blood begins to pound in my ears at the injustice of his imprisonment. I don't care what the general said, because in my eyes Joe is a hero. How could they kill him for loving his family? How is that a crime? I grind my teeth with frustration and clench my fists, digging my nails into the palms of my hands.

I try to maintain composure as Suzie leads us through the dusty, claustrophobic centre of Panama, where rusty metal shipping containers are crammed in closely, lining narrow alleyways in all directions. With these ominous makeshift buildings towering over us, and no greenery in sight, you could almost forget that there is a lush green forest on the other side of the compound walls. I can't help but wonder how they got these things into Panama in the first place.

The further we go into this dizzying maze, the more I begin to panic; we have turned so many corners now that I have lost my sense of direction. Apparently sensing my unease, Suzie says over her shoulder, "Don't worry, I'll draw you a map when we get back to my bunk."

Off-duty soldiers fill the narrow alleyways and glare at us as we pass by, clearly confused by our presence. A rowdy group of young men crowd around a rickety old table and gamble for cigarettes. As I try to keep my head down and not draw any attention to myself, I notice a few of the containers have been left wide open; some appear to be used as offices and others are used for storage.

With the smell of dismembered Infected still clinging to my boots and intimidating soldiers on every corner, I think I would rather be out in the forest with no supplies than be anywhere near this place. We turn another corner and finally leave the claustrophobic maze of containers, heading into a dusty, open clearing where row upon row of moss-green tents line the edge of the compound.

Suzie points ahead of her.

"Home sweet home. My tent is one of the smaller ones on the far side."

It seems that this vast, barren field is where the army trains their men and women; a group of roughly twenty soldiers are doing press-ups in the dirt while their superior is leaning over bellowing their reps. In the distance, another group is tirelessly running laps with huge backpacks strapped to their shoulders. As we walk past them, Suzie informs us that the backpacks are completely filled with rocks.

When we finally arrive at the tent that Suzie calls home, she pulls back the entrance to reveal six uniform bunk beds; each bed has been made to perfection without so much as a crease in the linen. The tent is void of any personal belongings other than a metal trunk for each bed in the tent.

To our relief, all the beds are currently empty, giving us some welcome privacy; hopefully we can finally understand what the hell is going on. Suzie paces back and forth, looking nervous, and shakily runs her hands through her short blonde hair.

Becoming impatient, Will steps towards her. "So, do you wanna tell us what the deal is here?"

She stops in her tracks and places her hands on her hips. "Okay, so the reason that Joe said that you can trust me is that he was the lieutenant in my squad when I first joined the army." She pauses momentarily and gestures to Tommy and me.

"And not only did I help rescue his niece and nephew from the Infected, but I also helped him escape from the military."

We stand there slack-jawed and continue to stare at Suzie. She folds her arms over her chest as she lets this new information sink in.

Attempting to ease the tension she quips, "You guys have grown up a lot since the last time I saw you!"

I shake my head in utter disbelief and confirm, "So hang on a minute, you guys know each other?"

Nodding her head, she smiles at me. "Oh, I know him well! I would have gone to hell and back for that man... Everyone in his squad had a huge amount of respect for Joe. We all still do." Smiling a sad smile at us, she continues, "Well, those of us that are left that is."

Feeling a little hopeful I ask, "So if you helped us once, can you help us again?"

Suzie puffs out her cheeks. "I don't think that's even remotely possible. You guys have only seen a small percentage of this place. This compound is huge! Not to mention the kind of security we have here… I seriously doubt that we could do this by ourselves without getting caught. I mean no offence, guys, I'm sure Joe has trained you well, but you're not going to be able to stand up against some of the soldiers stationed here."

She begins to pace again and verbalises her thought process. "Even if I could find someone that would be willing to help break Joe out – and that's a big IF by the way – we are essentially asking them to take part in a mutiny and potentially kill their fellow soldiers for Joe."

She stops pacing once more and shakes her head. "I would be giving up everything and risking my life – you understand that, right?"

With the grim reality sinking in, I beg, "Look, I know I'm asking a lot—"

She scoffs. "A lot doesn't even begin to cover it, sweetheart."

I give her a measured look and repeat, "I know I'm asking a lot, and you have done so much for us already, but I have to try. If you don't help us, we will try something without you, and who knows what the general will do to us…"

She begins to chew her bottom lip. "I'm not promising anything right now. I need to process all of this and sleep on it. Joe's trial will probably be in three days, two at the earliest, so we have a little time to think this through. You guys need to just hold tight, not do anything stupid and keep your heads down. I'll try and find out tonight when the trial is going to be."

Will looks to Suzie and narrows his eyes. "So, what will happen if they find him guilty?"

She opens her mouth to respond, but I quickly interject, "They will probably just keep him locked up… right?"

My eyes widen and my shoulders become tense as she looks at me curiously. I subtly shake my head and silently plead for her to go along with my lie. Nodding her head at us both, she says, "I don't know what will happen to him."

I exhale with relief as Will looks at me with a sideways glance. Luckily for me, he doesn't force the subject any further. Trying to push past my awkwardness, I quickly change the subject.

"You mentioned before that we need to keep our heads down, but what are the chances of Tommy *not* having a medical while we are here?"

Suzie stares at us determinedly. "Tommy must absolutely have his medical. It's going to be hard enough for me to try and help Joe without getting busted, but if I start to question this too, people will get suspicious of my involvement. In the next few days, I need to distance myself from you guys as much as possible, and you need to just play the game and do as you're told, which includes Tommy having a medical examination."

I nod my head and realise that I am pushing my luck. Suzie looks at Tommy and questions, "What's the big deal about a medical anyway? Is there something that you guys aren't telling me?"

Another lie easily forms at my lips: "Tommy is scared of needles. He gets sick and passes out – he's been through so much already today."

Suzie rolls her eyes at us and speaks to Tommy directly. "Well, my man, you're going to need to toughen up and take one for the team I'm afraid."

Tommy lowers his gaze, clearly uncomfortable. I wrap my arm around his shoulders in response. "Guess I'll just have to hold his hand then, huh?"

She smiles at me before she ruffles Tommy's hair. "I'm afraid so, champ!"

Suzie briefly looks at the battered watch on her wrist. "Right. I'm on guard duty in the next fifteen minutes, so you guys can just hang out here until I'm back for dinner in a few hours." She gestures in front of her. "This is my bunk here, and the one next to it is currently unoccupied, so you guys can sleep here, but unfortunately there are only two beds between the three of you…"

Will and I instantly look at each other, filled with awkwardness. Suzie stares at us, noticing the tension.

"It's up to you guys how you sort out the sleeping arrangements, but I would suggest that Alyx and Tommy share a bed and Will has the other one?"

Feeling my cheeks blush, I nod my head a little too quickly.

"Yep, sounds like a good idea."

Smiling at us, she heads towards the front of the tent. She pauses and grabs a small pad of paper out of her pocket and begins to scribble something down on it.

"Here's a very basic map of where a few things are like toilets and stuff. There are a couple of books in that trunk at the back; I'm sure Colt won't mind if you borrow them. Oh, and stay out of trouble, yeah?"

We all thank her as she quickly jogs out of the tent, leaving us alone to fend for ourselves. Will grins at us as he climbs up to the top bunk.

"Shotgun!"

I slump on the bottom bunk with my head in my hands and mumble, "Whatever you want…"

Will lies down with his hands behind his head. "We'll get him back, Ally. I promise we won't leave unless he's with us."

Feeling less doubtful, I say, "I think we're going to need a miracle to somehow sneak him out. I just don't understand why Joe would come to a place like this. Why would he risk getting caught?"

Leaning over the edge of the bunk he stares at me earnestly.

"Isn't it obvious? He did it for you guys. It was a calculated risk. He decided that saving Tommy was more important than the risk of potentially getting caught."

Sighing wearily, I kick off my boots and lie down on the bed, feeling physically exhausted. My limbs begin to ache from the battle with the Infected, making me feel as though I could sleep for a week. As I close my eyes, the image of Joe being dragged away by those soldiers whirls to the forefront of my mind. I grit my teeth as a feeling of defiance spreads through me. All those years ago, Joe saved Tommy and me from the brink of death – now it's time to repay the favour.

WE'RE JUST FRIENDS

Tommy and Will fell asleep shortly after Suzie left for her guard duty. With Joe's life hanging precariously in the balance, not to mention the fact that I had lied to Will, Tommy and Suzie, I have no chance of sleeping anytime soon. I did try to switch off for a while, but Tommy swiftly kicked me out of bed with all the tossing and turning. With sleep evading me, I decide to take myself outside the front of the tent, sprawl out on the dusty ground, prop my head up on my rucksack and bask in the afternoon sun with my eyes closed.

In the distance, men and women continue to train relentlessly under the strict supervision of a formidable man screaming at them to keep pushing. The rhythmic sound of boots thumping monotonously on solid ground is bizarrely soothing. I wonder if Suzie has to train like this under supervision? I get the impression that she is the lieutenant in her squad. Do the senior men and women in the army have to train at this level too? I decide to make a mental note to ask her that later. Taking in a deep breath, I attempt to clear my chaotic mind and focus on the humdrum of the soldiers training around me, and let the sun's warmth ease my aching muscles.

As I let my mind wander, I hear the sound of footsteps approaching from behind and then stop abruptly near my head. With my eyes still closed, I assume that it's Will.

"You're blocking out my sun."

A male voice responds, but it doesn't belong to Will. "Nice to meet you too."

Caught off guard, my eyes fling open to be greeted by the glaring sun; I bring my hand up to shield my face and squint through my fingers. As I clumsily push myself up into a seated position, I say, "Oh sorry, I thought you were someone else."

With my eyes fully open now, I am confronted by a young soldier in his early twenties, with messy dark brown hair and grey eyes. He stares at me quizzically as I dust myself down, desperately trying to regain some composure. A smile quivers at the corner of his smooth lips as I try to remain cool.

Raising his eyebrows at me, he crosses his muscular arms over his chest, making his already tight black t-shirt even tighter. As the sleeves of his t-shirt begin to ride up his tanned arms, I notice the bottom of a black tattoo peeping out from underneath. With a serious expression, he raises his chin and stares at me intensely, making my heart flutter in my chest.

He murmurs with a gravelly voice, "Sorry to disappoint you."

Not waiting for a response, he casually begins to walk towards the tent. Feeling a little indignant at his approach, I stand up to confront him.

"Is that it? You're not even going to introduce yourself?"

As soon as the words leave my mouth, I am surprised by

my own boldness. He turns around slowly as his grey eyes instantly lock onto mine. Placing my hands on my hips, I hold my head high to exude confidence. He considers me with curiosity.

"I'm Colt… and you're the one that told me to get out of your way."

Narrowing my eyes at him I snap, "Well, I already apologised for that!"

He nods his head coolly. "Okay… apology accepted."

Colt turns his back on me once more and heads for the entrance of the tent. With Tommy and Will still sound asleep, I step towards him and grab his wrist before he enters. He instantly looks down at my hand and seems surprised by my touch. Feeling a little embarrassed, I quickly let go.

"My brother Tommy and my friend Will are both sleeping in the spare bunk; Suzie said it was okay." I try to regain the upper hand. "And seeing as you're too rude to ask, I'm Alyx."

A look of mild amusement flashes across his face. "I'm going to grab my stuff to take a shower."

He finally disappears into the tent this time, leaving me alone outside. As soon as he's out of sight, I sigh heavily with frustration and then quickly run my fingers through my tangled hair.

After a few minutes, Colt strolls out the front of the tent with a black bag in his hand and a towel slung over his shoulder. Without stopping to talk to me, he says over his shoulder,

"See you around, Alyx."

I open my mouth to respond with something sarcastic, but before I can think of anything smart, he is halfway across the field. I am so consumed by my own thoughts that the sound of Will's voice behind me makes me jump.

"Who's that?"

I clutch my chest. "Jeez, Will, you scared the hell out of me!"

Rubbing his hands over his face, he stands next to me as I continue to watch Colt walk away from us. Will looks at me out of the corner of his eye.

"How long have I been out for?"

Finally prying my eyes away from Colt, I look at Will and smile at his cute bed hair.

"Erm, a few hours? Suzie will be back soon."

Nodding his head, he stifles a yawn with the back of his hand. "Man, that was a good power nap!"

With Tommy still asleep, I seize the opportunity to inform Will of the actual punishment for deserting. I hate keeping secrets at the best of times, especially from Will.

Whispering hurriedly, I close the distance between us. "Okay, so while Tommy is still asleep, I need to tell you something."

A creaking noise from the bunk bed stops me from continuing any further. I exhale with irritation and shake my head apologetically at Will. Moments later, a very bleary-eyed Tommy pulls back the entrance to the tent and joins us outside.

"What's going on?"

I silently curse under my breath for forgetting about Tommy's new hearing abilities. Smiling at him awkwardly, I say, "Nothing important."

Fortunately, I notice that Suzie is approaching from the other side of the field, which is a welcome distraction from any further questions from Tommy. She smiles at us sweetly as she approaches, but from the look in her eyes she's mentally exhausted.

"Glad to see that you managed to stay out of trouble," she says.

Will grins at her lopsidedly. "So far so good!"

She guides us all back inside the tent before she continues. "Okay, guys, dinner in the mess tent is served in an hour, so you need to get yourselves cleaned up and looking presentable. I have informed my captain that you're staying here with me, and Tommy's medical will be at nine o'clock tomorrow morning."

Suzie turns to Tommy and looks concerned. "Usually you're not allowed to have anyone go to the medical with you; however, as you are a minor and Alyx is technically your guardian in the absence of Joe, Alyx has clearance to attend with you, so you don't have to be so worried."

My stomach flips with guilt as a look of genuine concern spreads across her face. Tommy mumbles a thank you and then averts his gaze from her. She places her hand on his shoulder and stares at him earnestly before continuing, "Okay, so I still don't know when Joe's trial will be. I need to be careful who I get this information from. Also, as I said before, I need to distance myself from you all as much as possible and not draw any attention, so at dinner I suggest that you guys eat by yourselves."

Running her hand through her hair nervously, she added, "I know a guy in administration who has a soft spot for me, so I'll see if he's around at dinner tonight and try to find out about the trial, but no promises. We just need to be patient."

My heart sinks at the thought of Joe stuck in a cell somewhere in this compound, alone, waiting for his trial. I hope they are treating him humanely, but something tells me that the military doesn't take too kindly to deserters. I can't help but feel impatient.

"Thanks for all your help, Suzie, we appreciate it, and I understand that we need to play it safe, but at some point soon we need to figure out how we are going to attempt this. We don't know how much time we have left. What if the trial is tomorrow?"

She shakes her head. "I highly doubt that. I know the general, and he's an asshole, so he will want Joe to sweat it out for a couple of days before the trial, but I do agree that we need to be prepared as soon as possible."

Suzie puffs out her cheeks, looking weary. "I need time to mull it over by myself tonight and think about logistics, but to be honest, guys, I seriously wonder how we are going to manage to pull this off without getting killed."

Wandering over to her bunk, she starts to riffle through her belongings. "Let's go get ourselves cleaned up. After all, nothing is going to happen tonight. We can discuss plans tomorrow after Tommy's medical."

Tommy fidgets beside me, clearly as agitated as I am, but thankfully he manages to restrain himself. Suzie pulls out some spare clothes and hangs them up in front of me.

"These should fit. It's been a long time since I could squeeze my ass into these."

I look at her lean, muscular, athletic frame and wonder what the hell she is talking about, but I smile at her nonetheless and feel grateful for some clean clothes. She looks at Will and Tommy apologetically.

"None of my stuff will be good for you guys, but there should be some spare clothes in the lock-up near the showers."

Not wasting any time, we make our way back out of the tent and begin to cross the dusty training fields and head for the shower block. It's been so long since I've had a shower that I'm actually looking forward to it. As we turn a corner on the far side of the field, we pass a group of soldiers of various ages walking towards us with wet hair.

Suzie points to a container in front of us and confirms, "This is the lock-up with spare clothes and some provisions. Unfortunately, most of the good stuff is grabbed pretty quickly, but feel free to go through it all."

We all grab some boxes and start to rifle through them. In one box I happen across an old photo of a family on a beach and ask Suzie, "Where does this stuff come from?"

She shifts her weight uncomfortably. "From soldiers that have succumbed to the Infected usually."

A cold shiver trickles down my spine, which instantly makes me shudder in response. Will, on the other hand, seems completely unaffected by the thought of going through dead soldiers' belongings and continues to search the boxes. Thankfully, they find some suitable clothes quickly, and we all head for the showers. Suzie leads me into the women's side of the shower block as Tommy and Will wander off into the men's. As we walk through the entrance, Suzie grabs a bag that has some standard army-issue provisions, including soap, a toothbrush, toothpaste and a comb. She casually walks away from me, heads into a shower cubicle and points to her bag on the floor with a blank expression.

"Help yourself."

Her demeanour seems a little cold, but I quickly realise that she's probably putting on an act as we're not alone. I thank her meekly keeping my head down and disappear into a shower stall for some welcome privacy. As I turn on the tap, I can't help but grin as hot water instantly comes pouring out. I strip down quickly and jump in, taking full advantage of such a luxury.

As the hot water trickles down my back, my good mood quickly fades as my mind casts back to Joe, who is currently stuck in some awful prison cell waiting to die. A lump rises in my throat as a wave of guilt washes over me. How can I be enjoying myself when Joe is probably suffering right now? Taking in a shuddery breath, I focus on getting myself cleaned up quickly so that I can join the others and hopefully begin our plans to rescue Joe.

I dry myself off and quickly dress in Suzie's old clothes and wander out of the shower stall, catching a glimpse of my reflection in a full-length mirror. My long brown hair dangles down the centre of my back, making my tight black t-shirt a little wet. My camouflage khakis cling to my hips, giving me curves in places I didn't know I had. As I stare at myself in the mirror, feeling a little self-conscious, I can't help but tug at the hem of my t-shirt. These clothes are much tighter than I'm used to wearing.

Now that we are completely alone in the shower block, Suzie grins at me and sighs.

"Damn you're going to make the boys swoon tonight. I'm too old to be wearing stuff like that anymore."

I shake my head and wonder how someone as impressive as Suzie could possibly be envious of someone like me. Suzie is the kind of girl that could take on most guys in a fight and easily win, but somehow manage to keep her hair perfectly styled in the process. She passes me a small tub of something and then continues to dry her hair with a towel.

"That stuff is like gold dust, so use it sparingly. I found it in an abandoned village during a tour a few months back. It's coconut oil. You can use a little on your hair and on your skin."

As I run the coconut oil through my hair and rub a little on my face and arms, I notice that Suzie has cleaned my boots to near perfect condition. Before I have time to thank her, she continues, "So have you met Colt yet?"

Trying to keep my expression even, I shrug. "Oh, him? Yeah, he stopped by before heading to the showers."

Suzie eyes me suspiciously. "Nice guy when you get to know him… but he can be a little intense sometimes."

I can't help but scoff in response. "Well, Colt wasn't nice to me."

She smiles at me sympathetically. "Okay, good, because the boy is a heartbreaker. All the new recruits fall for him, and he always loses interest, so you want to stay clear of him."

Feeling a little flustered, I open my mouth to speak but she quickly cuts me off. "Just trust me on this one, Alyx… and besides, Will clearly has a thing for you."

My cheeks flush bright red as I stumble over my words. "Oh, we're just friends!"

Smiling at me cheekily, she says, "Yeah, sure you are."

Suzie stuffs her belongings into her bag and drops her towel into a bin in the corner. Shoving her boots on, she ties her laces speedily and then quickly ushers me outside. Tommy stands awkwardly to one side waiting for us, wearing clothes that look a little too big for his frame. Will, on the other hand, leans lazily against a container, wearing a black t-shirt and khakis similar to mine. The colours in the camouflage complement his glistening green eyes as I quickly realise that he looks at home in a military uniform.

As soon as I approach Will, he instantly straightens with a look of surprise on his face; he stares at me intensely and his breath catches in his throat. Suzie begins to walk away from us, back across the field, with a smug expression on her face. "Just friends, huh?"

SO MUCH FOR KEEPING A LOW PROFILE

Tommy hurriedly follows Suzie away from the showers, leaving Will and I staring at each other in awkward silence. On the first day that we arrived at Merope, completely traumatised following the death of my parents, two of the first people that I remember greeting us at the gates were Will and his mum. He stood holding her hand and stared at us filled with curiosity, with his round green eyes and messy golden hair.

I can only imagine how we must have looked: two frightened children, probably filthy dirty and malnourished, being carried by a battle-weary Joe. To a young Will, who had not yet experienced the horrors outside the world of Merope, we must have appeared feral in comparison.

Despite our appearance on that day, I saw a glimmer of the man that he was destined to become. Most children probably would have been scared by our arrival, but not Will. He toddled up to us, held out his hand to Joe and presented a delicately carved wooden fish to him. That was the first time that I had seen Joe smile since the day that he rescued us from the Infected. He thanked Will before he scurried off to hide behind his mum once more.

Will later told me that fish was his favourite toy at the time, one that his late father had carved himself. As I stare into Will's green eyes now, I can't help but feel like that little girl once more, feeling a mixture of fear and anticipation of what is yet to come.

Will shakes his head and raises his eyebrows at me. "You look… good. You look great, actually."

Trying to make light of the tension building between us I joke, "Wow, Will, that almost sounded like a compliment!"

He grins at me. "You're welcome, and don't get used to it, by the way!"

In the distance, Suzie whistles at us to hurry up. Will laughs heartily as he lazily drapes his arm over my shoulders. As soon as we approach Suzie, I notice that her body language has changed again with other soldiers in close proximity; she glares at us angrily and emanates impatience with her hands firmly planted on her hips.

"I'm not your babysitter, okay, so don't make me wait. Otherwise next time you can go hungry!"

Will instantly drops his arm from my shoulders like a naughty schoolboy and straightens his stance reflexively. Giving us a curt nod, Suzie marches into the tent, leaving us to fend for ourselves once more. As soon as we walk through the threshold, the deafening noise of mindless chatter and metal dishes clanging on tables makes me wince. Tommy stares at me with wild eyes, not surprisingly overwhelmed. Noticing his expression, I speak in a lowered voice and gently cup his cheek.

"Everything is okay. All we need to do is eat quickly and

get the hell out of here. If it's too much, let me know and we can leave at any time."

His shoulders visibly relax following my reassurance, so I quickly grab his hand and head towards the food service. As we join the back of the line, soldiers around us stare at us quizzically, clearly confused by our presence. A group nearby huddles together and speaks in hushed tones; I hear one of them mention Joe's name.

With the combination of soldiers filling every square inch of the tent, hot food being served and Suzie's ridiculously tight clothes, I start to feel a little dizzy. Trying to cool down, I gather my thick brown hair up from my shoulders and temporarily hold it into a messy bun at the nape of my neck, letting the air circulate underneath.

Colt is sitting with a group of soldiers who are laughing and joking around him. At first sight, he seems to be uninterested or bored by their company; however, from the expression on his face, he actually seems to be deep in thought and even preoccupied by something.

As soon as he notices us waiting in the queue, he stares at me intensely and absentmindedly plays with his food. A smile quivers at the corner of his mouth as he quickly turns away and finally starts to chat to the guy sitting next to him.

There's something about Colt that distinctly separates him from those around him. Some people could mistake his mannerisms as arrogant, but after watching him, he seems complicated, and as Suzie described earlier, even a little intense. Will says something beside me, but I'm too distracted by Colt to listen. Becoming impatient, Will places his hand on my arm.

"Did you hear what I said?"

Feeling a little flustered, I mumble, "Sorry, just feeling a bit anxious today. That's Colt – the guy I met earlier… He was kind of a jerk to me."

Raising his chin, he places his hand on the small of my back defensively and almost puffs out his chest.

"Do I need to say something to him?"

My eyes suddenly widen in response. "What? No! Are you crazy? Besides, he didn't do anything that bad. He was just a little off with me that's all…"

Will stares at him, clearly eyeing him up as I try to change the subject. "Look, we don't want to be drawing any more attention to ourselves anyway, seeing as I've probably done enough damage already by punching Bobby in the nose."

Will grins at me and points directly at Bobby, who has been sulkily glaring at us ever since we entered. "Come on, Ally, that was funny! The sleazebag deserved it!"

Bobby jumps to his feet, following Will's blatant gesture, and slowly begins to walk over to us.

Will automatically takes a protective stance in front of me and mumbles, "Looks like our friend here isn't worried about drawing any attention."

I curse under my breath. "So much for keeping a low profile…"

Feeling indignant that this creep is going to start something with me again, I push my way past Will despite his protests and go to meet Bobby first. Will reluctantly stays back and firmly places his hand on Tommy's shoulder, not taking any chances. Staring at me with hateful eyes, Bobby practically spits as he approaches.

"You have some nerve showing up here, don't you?"

Not being able to help myself I point to his black eye and bruised nose. "Did you want me to even it up by punching you in the other eye?"

A group of soldiers nearby burst out laughing as Bobby quickly closes the distance between us. "You better watch your back, sweetheart. I'll get you when there's no one around to hear you scream."

Colt is suddenly behind Bobby in a flash and grabs him by the shoulder with gritted teeth. "Leave her alone!"

Bobby spins around and shoves him in the chest without much success; Bobby is much smaller in comparison to Colt's lean muscular frame. Colt barely even flinches and simply stares at him with an unfazed icy glare.

With all the commotion, Suzie marches over and starts yelling at both of them and orders them out of the tent. Before he exits, Colt casts one final look at me over his shoulder then disappears outside.

Bobby, on the other hand, spits at the floor, to which Suzie screams, "That's another fifty push-ups, Private!"

I stand there wide-eyed, wondering what the hell had just happened. Did Colt just try to defend me? After the way he spoke to me earlier, I thought he seriously disliked me. The noise in the tent begins to rise again as the soldiers turn back to finish their meals.

Furrowing my brow, I say, "What the hell was that all about?"

Will shrugs his shoulders, clearly trying to brush it off. "This place is full of psychos. The sooner we get out of here the better."

A soldier serving food behind us shouts, "Next!"

I turn back round to see endless trays of hot food being served by four soldiers that clearly hate their jobs. As I stare at the delicious food laid out in front of us, all I can think about is Colt.

Will murmurs beside me, "Where the hell do they get all this food from? I don't remember seeing any agriculture in this place."

Will's question draws my attention. "Good point. Me neither…"

Back home in Merope, most of the time we had to survive on rations to some degree. During the winter when food supplies were scarce, times could get very hard. I remember one year when the harvest was particularly bad. Everyone in the whole town suffered the consequences, and there were some days where we only had a single meal. During the summer when fruit and vegetables were plentiful, we would already be planning for the winter ahead.

As I look at the endless trays brimming with food, my mind whirls with all the possibilities of where it could have been sourced from, all of which suddenly puts me on edge. With my hunger quickly disappearing before my eyes, the soldier serving food glares at me with impatience. I quickly point to the tray of roasted sweet potatoes and a selection of green vegetables.

Tommy stares at the food, overwhelmed and anxious, so I order him the same plate of food as mine. Will, on the other hand, has always loved his food, and if given the choice, would eat ten meals a day; it's probably to do with the fact that he's built like a Viking. Without the slightest hesitation he takes full advantage and fills his plate with a variety of meats, potatoes and vegetables.

We walk over to the far side of the tent to an empty table and begin to eat in silence. Suzie enters the tent once more with flushed cheeks without even glancing in our direction. Smiling sweetly, she sits down at a table with her fellow lieutenants and begins to chat to them animatedly. I hope she manages to find out the details of Joe's trial tonight. After everything that has happened with Bobby, the sooner we leave the better.

Lost in my own thoughts, I suddenly hear Tommy scoffing his food beside me; he's eating so quickly that he can't possibly be chewing any of it before he swallows. I grab his wrist tightly and yank the fork out of his hand. The last thing we need right now is anyone noticing Tommy.

"Stop that right now. If you keep eating like that, someone will notice and then we will be in serious trouble!"

Tommy lowers his gaze, looking visibly wounded. "I'm sorry, I just can't stop myself. Every time I see food, something happens inside me that I can't control."

I look at his sad eyes and instantly feel guilty for snapping at him.

"I'm sorry, Tommy. I didn't mean to be so aggressive. I know this is hard for you. It's hard for all of us, and with everything that's happened today, and with Joe gone, I'm just feeling a little overwhelmed, and I shouldn't have taken it out on you."

I smile at him to lighten the mood. "Maybe try and count your chews every time you eat? Maybe the distraction will slow you down?"

I pass the fork back to him as he nods his head meekly; he slowly cuts a small piece of sweet potato as a look of concentration spreads across his face. Looking a little happier he confirms, "It's actually helping."

I rub his back for reassurance. "Good, I'm glad."

The rest of the dinner thankfully passes by without any further dramas. Suzie stands up to leave and glances in our direction for the first time this evening, almost encouraging us to leave too. Not wasting any time, and anxious for further information, we follow her out in the hope that we can begin our plans to rescue Joe.

The stars twinkle in the clear night's sky as the moon illuminates our path back to the tent. In the distance, Bobby and Colt are running laps in the dusty field under the strict supervision of Suzie. She finally calls them in and dismisses them before marching over in our direction. Holding her hands up, she shakes her head in dismay.

"Sorry about Bobby earlier. You don't need to worry about him."

Feeling a little unsure of that, I nod my head in appreciation as Tommy suddenly interjects. "When can we see Joe? I want to see him now!"

Suzie looks at him sympathetically. "I'm sorry, buddy, but there's simply no way that you can see him tonight." She shifts her weight nervously before she continues, "But, I did manage to find out when his trial is…"

We all stare at her with bated breath.

"Joe's trial is at three o'clock tomorrow."

We stand slack-jawed and stare at her in disbelief. My heart races with panic as my hands begin to shake.

"Are you serious? I thought you said the general would make him sweat a couple of days?"

Suzie runs her hands through her short hair. "I

genuinely thought that he would do that – turns out that I was wrong."

Throwing my arms up, I say, "What the hell are we going to do? Tommy has his medical tomorrow at nine, and we have no idea how long that will take, and then we have to somehow rescue Joe?" My heart sinks into the pit of my stomach as the bleak reality sets in. "How are we going to pull this off?"

Will places his hand on my shoulder, trying to calm me down.

"Look, everything will be okay. We can stay up all night if we have to and make sure we have it all figured out, right, Suzie?"

We all turn to her with wide eyes and clenched fists; whatever the plan is, it heavily depends on Suzie, and from the expression on her face, she is fully aware of that. Sighing through gritted teeth, she stares at us filled with determination.

"Well, I guess this is a good time to tell you my suicide mission of a plan then, huh?"

THE SUICIDE MISSION

Before continuing any further, Suzie guides us all back inside the tent and closes the entrance behind us. She attempts to drag one of the metal trunks from the nearest bunk bed without much success. After adjusting her position, she leans heavily on one side and begins to push the seemingly immovable object until Will quickly steps in and helps drag it into the centre of the tent.

Suzie then quickly paces over to her own bunk bed, riffles through her personal belongings and drops a pile of random objects onto the centre of the trunk, including a comb, a couple of pens, a compass and a ball of string. Pointing to the objects now piled up on the trunk, Will picks up the ball of string.

"What's all this for?"

Suzie exhales loudly. "It's the best I can do. These objects will represent various people and locations to illustrate my plan."

Speaking hurriedly, she continues, "We probably only have thirty minutes before the rest of the squad comes back in here for the night, so just listen first and then ask questions later, got it?"

Nodding my head furiously, my heart pounds as we all

kneel in front of the trunk and Suzie begins to arrange her objects.

"Okay, so my plan has only one scenario following Joe's trial, and that is that he will be found guilty. If by some miracle he is found to be innocent, then he will be released from custody, so no rescue plan is required. But as it stands, I would say that I'm ninety-nine percent sure that Joe will be found guilty. That is the reality."

I quickly interject, not wanting to risk even a small possibility that he will meet his sentence, "But shouldn't we try and rescue him before he goes to trial?"

Glaring at me, she bites back her tongue. "Sweetheart, I know you're eager but please let me explain first, okay?"

Feeling dejected, I fiddle with my hair anxiously as Suzie puffs out her cheeks and continues once more. "As I was saying, my plan is on the assumption that Joe will be found guilty."

She pauses and grabs the edge of the trunk and ponders her words carefully.

"But before I go any further, Tommy and Will have to know what the punishment is for deserting… I know, Alyx, that you didn't want them to know for whatever reason, but this plan can't work unless we are all completely aligned. I don't want any secrets, okay? Especially as all our lives are at stake here, including Joe's."

Tommy and Will glare at me with narrowed eyes, making my heart sink with guilt. Feeling resigned I slowly turn to Tommy and hold his hands.

"Look, I haven't been completely honest because I didn't want to upset you…"

Tommy tenses and snatches his hands away from mine. I

bow my head before continuing, "I did it because I wanted to protect you, okay? So please focus on that before you react."

I raise my chin and stare into Tommy's eyes and hope that he can see the sincerity in mine. A part of me wants to maintain the lie, but I know that Suzie is right: they have to know the truth for any rescue plan to work. After all, if Tommy found out the punishment during the trial, any plans we may have had would have ended in total disaster.

As the words begin to form at my lips, I momentarily hesitate. By finally admitting the truth out loud, Joe's fate suddenly becomes a reality and is no longer some horrible nightmare. Trying to stop my voice from breaking I croak, "The punishment for deserting is death by firing squad."

Will's eyes widen as he sucks in a sharp breath. Tommy clenches his fists, making the veins pop in his forearms. He then jumps to his feet with crazy eyes as his face flushes bright red with rage. Trying to prevent the situation from escalating any further, I stand up next to him and gently reach out.

"Everything will be okay, Tommy. Just take a deep breath. Joe isn't going to die. I won't let that happen!"

Snarling at me, he begins to shake with anger. "How could you keep this from me!"

I tentatively take a step towards him and open my mouth to speak, but as soon as I close the distance, Tommy shoves me away. He brings up his clenched fist and slams it down on the metal trunk, scattering Suzie's belongings in every direction. Suzie stumbles back in shock and stares wide-eyed at the huge dent in the centre of the solid metal trunk.

She mutters, "What the…"

Will lunges at Tommy and grabs his arms to stop him from creating any more damage. With my own temper rising, I stand firmly and point my finger inches away from his face, trying to maintain his attention.

"This is exactly why I didn't tell you, Tommy!" I gesture at the trunk. "Look what you've done. How am I going to explain this? This doesn't just affect you, it affects all of us! Do you want to end up in jail like Joe, or even worse, in a lab somewhere?"

Realisation flashes across his face as he breathes deep, ragged breaths. Staring at him earnestly, I almost beg as he continues to struggle against Will.

"Please stop."

With one hand on her chest, trying to steady herself, Suzie points directly at the dent and demands, "Someone needs to tell me what's going on!"

At the sound of her authoritative voice, Tommy finally starts to slow his breathing down to a normal rate, but his pupils remain dilated. I look to Will for support, but he gently shakes his head.

"There's no point trying to hide anything. Just tell her everything."

Suzie steps towards me assertively. "Tell me right now, or you guys are on your own."

Holding my hands up in admission, I sigh heavily, feeling mentally exhausted; I can't help but wonder when this awful day is going to be over. Will releases Tommy as I turn to address Suzie.

"Okay, let me explain. There's no real easy way to say this, so I'm just going to say it, but please don't freak out… Tommy was infected."

Taking another step back, she stares at me like I'm crazy.

"What do you mean he was infected? How is that even possible?"

At that moment, Colt bursts through the tent door without warning.

"Are you okay, Lieutenant? I heard—"

Colt absorbs the scene unfolding in front of his eyes and finally notices the dent in the metal trunk. Almost stumbling over my words I blurt, "It's not what it looks like."

Colt slowly looks at me and then points at the dented trunk.

"And what is this supposed to look like?"

Cursing under my breath, I mumble to myself, "Could this day get any worse…?"

Suzie forces a smile at Colt. "Everything is fine. It's all under control."

"With all due respect, Lieutenant, I'm not sure it is."

Suzie sighs heavily, places her hands on her hips to take charge and addresses all of us. "You can trust Colt as much as you can trust me. I've known Colt since he was a baby and he's like family to me. If we're lucky, he may be willing to help us out, and if he's not, I know wholeheartedly that he wouldn't say anything, right, Colt?"

He nods his head and stares at her curiously as she continues, "We don't have much time before the rest of the squad turns up tonight, so you may as well just tell us everything from the beginning and then Colt can decide if he's in or not."

I stare at Will and shrug my shoulders, feeling as though I have been backed into a corner. As I look between Colt, Suzie and finally Tommy, I attempt to formulate a response in my mind, but as soon as I open my mouth to speak, laughter begins to bubble inside my chest at the ridiculousness of the situation. You know things are really bad when all you can do is laugh. Tears begin to stream down my face as I begin to giggle uncontrollably. Will steps towards me, filled with concern.

"What's going on? Are you okay?"

Will's words only make me laugh even more. Between snorts, I wipe away my tears with the back of my hand.

"Are you serious? Am I okay? Let me think about that… am I okay? I think the answer to that question is no, I'm not!"

Everyone stands in awkward silence, staring at me, as I throw my arms up in dismay and continue to babble. "Everything is so screwed up! When I started to think of all the awful things that have happened to us in the last two days, I couldn't decide whether to laugh or cry… and it seems I decided to do both!"

I glance sideways and notice that Colt is staring at me with genuine concern; maybe I've finally lost my mind. Will lowers his voice and quickly pulls me into a tight hug, turning my back on Colt.

"I know it feels bad right now, but we need to focus on Joe." Looking over at Suzie and then finally at Colt, he says, "Joe trusts Suzie… and if Suzie trusts Colt, then I think we should too – even if he was an asshole to you earlier."

Turning back to me, he delicately lifts my chin up so that he can maintain eye contact. As he tenderly wipes away the salty dampness from my cheeks, for a brief moment I thought that he might lean down to kiss me. Breaking the tension, Colt takes a step forward to respond to Will's accusation, but Suzie puts her arm out to stop him.

"Leave it, Colt. I don't think my nerve endings can take anymore right now. Alyx, I know you've been through a lot, but the more we stand here staring at each other, the less time we have to figure this all out."

Suzie's words snap my mind back into focus as Will takes a step away from me and then glares at Colt in the process. I press my fingers into my temples and wince in pain as a tension headache begins to throb. Exhaling with exhaustion, I cast my mind back and begin to tell the story of how Joe rescued us from the Infected when we were kids, quickly followed by how Tommy became infected.

"So that's the reason we came to this damn place – we hoped to stock up and then head to Alhena to hopefully get help for Tommy and maybe find out why he has all these 'abilities'… but then Joe got arrested and, well, you know the rest."

Colt and Suzie stare at me wide-eyed, trying to process all of this information. Colt shakes his head and points at Tommy.

"So, this kid survived infection, is that what you're saying?"

"He was definitely infected. He had the black veins, the fever, the sickness… everything."

"And now he has abilities? What kind of abilities?"

Shifting my weight uneasily, I say, "So far that we know of, he has excellent hearing and sense of smell, super strength… hence the dent."

Will interjects, "But he also has an insatiable hunger too, and his emotions are all over the place."

Suzie stares at him, looking somewhere between frightened and horrified. "So I assume this is the reason that you didn't want him to have the medical?"

"As I said earlier, we don't fully understand how this has even happened, and we want to make sure that he gets help… and that the wrong people don't find out about him. Tommy could be the key to everything. He could be the cure."

Will steps forward. "Or he could still be infected and turn at any moment."

I can't help but flinch at the harsh reality of Will's words. Lowering my gaze slightly, I cross my arms over my chest defensively and attempt to steady my breathing. Noticing my change in body language, Colt stares at me intensely with his steely grey eyes.

"Count me in."

Suzie whips her head round. "You do realise what is at stake here? This will be the end of your military career, not to mention the fact that we could all die in the process?"

Without breaking her gaze, he says, "If there's even a remote possibility that this kid could be the cure for all of this, then I want in."

A smile creeps at the corner of her mouth in approval. "Okay, well, now that everything is out in the open, we have about five minutes to go through the plan…if we're lucky."

To make amends, Tommy dashes around and collects all of Suzie's belongings from the floor and hands them back to her nervously. She thanks him before she gathers us around the trunk once more.

"Unfortunately, Tommy still needs to have his medical tomorrow because not only will it draw unnecessary attention if I question his requirement to have one, but Tommy's medical is integral to my plan. Alyx, I'm sure you can figure out a way to steal any samples they collect from Tommy."

Holding my hand up, I say, "It's okay. Don't worry, I'll figure something out. What is it that you need us to do?"

Suzie fiddles with her compass absentmindedly. "You need to steal a key card from one of the guards when you're down in the labs for Tommy's medical. There's a huge part of this complex that you haven't even seen yet, and that's because it's underground. This place isn't just a military base. We have an entire research facility, including agricultural fields where they are able to grow crops in a scientifically controlled environment, also known as pharming."

At the words 'research facility' panic begins to rise in my chest. "That's the last place that we want Tommy to go to! It was bad enough when I thought some military doctor would be taking blood from him, but now you're saying that we are literally sitting on top of a huge research facility? I bet they would love to make Tommy a lab rat!"

Biting her lip anxiously, Suzie says, "I know this is less than ideal, but I should also add that this is where Joe is being held prisoner. As far as I'm aware, they aren't doing any medical research down there. It's mostly weapons, agriculture, that kind of thing."

Exhaling loudly, I try to ignore the sense of dread in the pit of my stomach. "Okay, so let's assume that I manage to steal Tommy's samples and a guard's key card without getting caught – what's next?"

Suzie swallows hard and runs her hands through her short blonde hair.

"Assuming that both of those things happen without any hiccups, after Joe's trial there will be a small window between the end of the trial and when his sentence is carried out. At that point, we break into the lab using the stolen key card and escape with Joe through the ventilation system that's used for the pharming, which should take us far away from this place. However, I'm pretty sure they use the ventilation systems to distribute chemicals onto the crops, not to mention that the fans generate excess noise."

Colt nods his head and sets his jaw firmly as he murmurs, "That's why the tunnels for the ventilation system go for miles because they create so much noise. Every couple of weeks, they take us out on a clean-up exercise at the tunnel exit to reduce the number of Infected."

Suzie stares at us with wide eyes. "So, providing that we don't get poisoned by toxic fumes on the escape route, at the end of the mission, we will probably be met by an army of Infected."

Will stares at Suzie with a deadpan expression. "So, you weren't kidding when you said your plan was a suicide mission then, huh?"

MONSTER IN THE DARKNESS

The other eight members of the squad appeared shortly after Suzie had explained the layout of the lab in detail, including where Joe is currently being held prisoner. Tommy even had time to flatten the metal trunk to avoid any difficult questions. It's clear from the squad's attitude towards Suzie that they all have the upmost respect for their lieutenant.

When she explained to them that we would be staying the night, not a single solider questioned her authority, and in fact, many of them were exceedingly polite to us. Five of the soldiers, three men and two women, crawled into their respective bunk beds to read and have continued to lie there quietly ever since, while three young guys similar in age to Colt huddle together playing cards at the far end. The mood in the tent is peaceful, which is a welcome relief from the emotional rollercoaster that we have experienced today.

Colt lies on his bunk bed reading a tatty old book that looks as though it has seen better days. Every now and then, I catch him glancing over in my direction. Tommy and I lie on our backs and try to lighten the mood by recalling funny stories from our childhood, whereas Will lies on the top bunk with his hands behind his head, staring at the roof of the tent. He seems distant and preoccupied, which is very unusual for him.

Suzie, on the other hand, has been unable to sit still since the discussion of our plan. She finally jumps up from her bunk bed and dims the main light, encouraging the rest of the squad to turn in for the night. With the lights down low, I take the opportunity to get undressed and search for something more suitable to wear, rather than Suzie's ridiculously tight military uniform. As I rifle through my meagre belongings, I find one of Joe's favourite shirts crumpled at the bottom of my pack. I pull it out shakily and hold it against my chest as tears begin to blur my vision. I quickly strip off my clothes, suddenly not caring if any of the soldiers witness it, and pull the shirt over my head, letting Joe's scent encapsulate me.

Feeling physically and emotionally exhausted, I crawl into the bottom bunk, quickly followed by Tommy. He nuzzles his head into the nook of my shoulder and takes in a deep breath, letting his shoulders relax. As I close my eyes, my mind is filled with Joe's image as a single tear trickles down my cheek.

Tommy whispers in the darkness, "Sorry about earlier. I didn't mean to get so angry about Joe. I know that you're only worried about me."

Ruffling his hair, I kiss the top of his head and feel grateful that after everything that has happened, amazingly, I still have my little brother at my side.

Whispering in his ear, I say, "No I'm sorry. I should've told you in private earlier, but things got a bit crazy. I know you're not a kid anymore, but I can't help but feel overly protective. I'm just scared to death that I'll lose you again, especially now that Joe has been arrested. I'm terrified that I'll end up losing both of you."

Tommy snuggles me tighter. "We are all leaving this place together as a family, because I believe in you, Alyx."

A lump begins to rise in my throat as I ponder his words. I hope with all my heart that his sentiment comes true. I feel Tommy relax beside me and start to breathe slow, rhythmic breaths, which in itself, is strangely soothing. As I let my mind drift, I try to expel all the worries that are currently plaguing me and focus on happy memories from back home. Not surprisingly, within minutes I fall fast asleep.

I wake in the early hours of the morning, feeling stiff and uncomfortable from heavy sleep. Tommy's arm is draped over my chest as he continues to breathe hot, moist air into the crook of my neck. With Tommy still lying on me and my aching limbs, I have a sudden urge to get some fresh air.

Rubbing my bleary eyes, I carefully slide out of the bed and tiptoe barefoot out the front of the tent, wearing nothing but Joe's shirt. The compound is eerily quiet as a warm breeze blows lazily across the dusty training field; the moon shines brightly in the clear night sky as a handful of soldiers continue their guard duty on the towering walls.

In the distance, lights surrounding the perimeter flicker, making the shadows come alive in the darkness. A feeling of unease creeps through me, making the hairs prickle on the back of my neck. I take a deep breath and run my fingers through my hair, reminding myself that the monsters are on the other side of these formidable walls. I close my eyes and enjoy a rare moment of solitude before the rescue mission tomorrow; the proverbial calm before the storm.

Out of the darkness, a hand clamps firmly over my mouth, catching me completely off guard. I try to scramble away as an arm wraps tightly around my throat, closing off my airway. As adrenaline surges through me, I dig my fingernails into his forearms and kick out furiously like a wild animal, but to no avail. My attacker grunts behind me and begins to drag me away from the safety of the tent, scraping my bare legs on the dusty floor.

My vision begins to swim as he hisses in my ear, "Silly girl out here in the dark by yourself. I did try and warn you, darlin'… No one can save you now!"

At the sound of Bobby's voice, panic consumes me. It turns out that I was very wrong – there are monsters on this side of the wall too. My legs feel like lead as my grip loosens on his forearm. I take in one last shuddery breath as my eyes roll into the back of my head, sending me into a black hole of unconsciousness.

My eyes flutter open as a cold sensation begins to creep into my bones. Bobby sits in the corner of the shipping container and stares at me hungrily. I try to push myself up into a seated position without much success. My wrists and ankles are bound together tightly, heavily restricting my movements. I quickly scan my surroundings to find my escape route as a creepy smile stretches across his face.

Gritting my teeth, I steady my breathing to stop overwhelming panic from consuming my thoughts; all I need to do is clear my mind and bide my time. I can get out of this, I know I can. Joe always told me that fear can be your biggest weakness and anything could be used as a potential weapon. Ironically, when he taught me that he was referring to the Infected, not to psychopaths like Bobby.

Raising my chin, I take a deep breath and stare at him coldly. "Hello, Bobby."

He raises his arm and aims a pistol at my head.

"Hello, darlin'. Now I know your pretty little head is probably trying to figure out how you're getting out of this one, but unfortunately, there is no way out. My buddies on watch duty are keeping an eye out for any of your so-called friends that may try to interrupt us."

I continue to stare at Bobby with a blank expression. Something tells me that this sicko will enjoy this even more if I appear to be frightened. I shrug my shoulders.

"And what exactly would they be interrupting, Bobby? If you're going to kill me, just get it over with… but I should warn you, Will and Suzie will kill you when they find out what you have done."

Shaking his head, he tuts under his breath. "Oh, darlin', I ain't going to kill you… not at first anyway. After we have finished, however, you will be begging me to put a bullet in your head."

Swallowing hard, I maintain eye contact as my mind continues to race. I need to distract him as I continue to loosen the ropes secured around my wrists.

"You know what, Bobby? I'm not scared of you. I just feel bad for you…"

Gritting his teeth, he glares at me. "You watch your mouth now!"

Ignoring him I push on. "I mean, you must be really desperate if the only way you can get a girl is to tie them up."

He jumps to his feet and steps towards me. "I'm warning you!"

"What happened to you to make you this pathetic?"

As soon as the words leave my mouth, he lunges forward and slams into me, knocking the breath out of my lungs. I curse myself for pushing it too far too soon. He cracks my head on the metal floor as his face flushes bright red with rage. With all the commotion, I attempt to wriggle away from him, but he swiftly digs the barrel of his gun firmly into the middle of my forehead.

"One more word and I'll blow your pretty little head off!"

With the gun still pressed to my forehead, he leans over, grabs my wrists with his free hand and slams them into the floor above my head, sending shooting pains up my arms. I lay there frozen as he begins to close the distance between us. Bobby slowly leans down and whispers in my ear, as he reaches between my legs and grazes the barrel of the gun up my inner thigh.

"I'm going to enjoy this."

Swallowing back bile, tears begin to sting my eyes as I repeat the mantra 'I can survive this' over and over in my mind. The acrid smell of cigarettes and sweat fills my senses as my muscles tense at his touch. He leans down once more and traces his tongue along my jawline and then slowly begins to kiss my neck.

He rips open Joe's shirt, popping all the buttons in the process, and then licks his lips at the sight of my black underwear. He clicks the gun's safety off and continues to point it steadily at my head.

"I'm going to take the ties off around your ankles. If you even so much as flinch, I'll start shootin'."

He tugs sharply at the ropes tied around my ankles but maintains eye contact in the process. I continue to keep my expression blank, even when my skin starts to throb from friction burn. He kneels over me, unzips his khakis and digs deep inside to try and reveal himself. Stifling back a sob, I bite my tongue and realise it's now or never.

He leans down once more and pulls at my panties as the gun wavers slightly in his hand. Seizing the opportunity, I bring my knees up sharply and kick him in the crotch. He instantly hunches forward and cries out in pain. Setting my jaw firmly, I take advantage of his vulnerability by swiftly headbutting him in the face, watching his already crooked nose explode with blood for the second time today. Bobby rolls off me, doubled over, swearing in agony.

I scramble to my feet and run towards the container door with my wrists still tightly bound. I pull at the handle furiously and quickly realise the damn thing is locked. Bobby spits blood on the floor and growls at me with red-stained teeth while I gnaw at the ropes around my wrists. Crying out in frustration, I continue to pull at the ties desperately as he slowly begins to climb to his feet.

Now out of time, I run at him and kick him square in the chest, slamming him against the wall; the gun flies out of his hand and skids across the floor in the process. Bouncing back, he roars with rage and shoves me onto the floor. As I try to scramble away, he grabs my ankles and begins to drag me towards him. He leans over me once more and punches me solidly in the face, making my vision instantly blurry.

Shaking my head, I bring my knee up onto his chest and flip him over onto his back, using his own weight against him. Before he can react, I whip my leg over his torso and then hook it firmly around his throat into a perfect choke hold, one that Joe would be proud of. Now all I need to do is strangle him unconscious; too much pressure and I'll kill him, not enough and he won't pass out.

His face becomes redder and redder the longer I squeeze his throat. He furiously claws at my thighs as he desperately tries to pry them away. His face turns purple as his eyes roll into the back of his head and he finally falls unconscious.

Filled with relief, I roll away from him to catch my breath. Tears begin to streak down my face as I start to sob uncontrollably. Pushing myself off the floor, I manage to untie my wrists using my teeth and grab Bobby's gun.

I stumble to the door and begin to slam my fists against the metal until they are bloody and raw. Screaming at the top of my lungs, I pray that someone will hear my cries. I briefly look over my shoulder to see that Bobby is beginning to stir.

Between my cries, I hear a male voice outside as I scream, "Help me!"

Colt's voice is like music to my ears. "Alyx? Is that you?"

Bobby begins to climb to his feet with his head in his hands. Stumbling over my words, I shout, "Colt, it's Bobby. He attacked me. He's going to kill me!"

Colt pulls at the door and curses loudly. "Bobby, I swear, if you touch her it will be the last thing that you ever do!" He continues to tug forcefully.

"Alyx, it's locked. I'll be back in two minutes!"

"No, don't leave me with him!"

Bobby starts to run towards me. I spin around, holding the gun firmly with two hands, and aim at his chest.

"Don't move!"

Grinning at me, he holds up his hands. "You don't seem like the kinda girl that could kill a human in cold blood!"

I glare at him with pure disgust. "You're right. I'm not the kinda girl that would kill a human in cold blood... but I have no problem shooting monsters like you!"

I adjust my aim and pull the trigger, sending a bullet tearing through his right shoulder. Bobby tumbles backwards as blood sprays behind him. The sound of the gun exploding in such a small space makes my ears scream with white noise.

Colt shouts from behind the door, "Alyx!"

Bobby screams in pain and my hands begin to shake. I stand over him and aim the gun at his head. So many good people have died since the start of this plague; this wretched man doesn't deserve to live.

As the door swings wide open, Colt rounds the corner and approaches with caution, quickly making sure the room is safe to enter. Taking in the scene around him, I turn and run into Colt's arms, nuzzling my head into his neck, and begin to sob uncontrollably.

He gently strokes my hair and keeps his gun firmly aimed at Bobby as he whispers in my ear, "You're alright now. Everything will be okay."

Through gritted teeth he says to Bobby, "I should kill you right now, you scumbag. But instead, I'm going to leave you right here to suffer!"

Guiding me towards the door, Colt walks backwards with his gun aimed at Bobby. Once outside, he slams the container door shut, stifling Bobby's screams. Cupping my face, he stares at me with his intense steely grey eyes.

"Are you hurt?"

I shake my head as I wipe the back of my hand across my tear-stained face. He takes off his t-shirt to reveal his muscular torso and gently pulls it over my head. Until now I had forgotten that I was wearing nothing but my underwear.

Feeling overcome with emotion, I throw my arms around his neck, suddenly grateful to be alive. At first Colt stiffens at my touch, but within seconds, I feel his muscles relax slowly, as he wraps his arms around my waist. With my heart in my throat, I pull back from the hug and look up at Colt through my eyelashes. He smiles a sad smile as he gently tucks my hair behind my ear.

"Are you sure you're not hurt?"

I shake my head meekly. "No, I'm okay, I think, but he did try to…"

My voice weakens when the word 'rape' comes to the forefront of my mind. Angry realisation flashes across Colt's face as he turns towards the container.

I rush forward and grab his hand.

"He didn't! He tried to… but he didn't!"

A smile creeps to the corner of my mouth. "I kicked him in the crotch so damn hard I don't think he will be doing that for a while!"

He stares at me intensely. "You're amazing, you know that, right? Most people would be a mess after what you've been through." I stare at him, feeling a little breathless as he continues with a gravelly voice. "And yet here you are like some beautiful warrior, taking on monsters like Bobby. You have no idea how perfect you are, do you?"

My cheeks flush bright red with embarrassment and my heart throbs in my chest. Without realising it, I close the distance between us, suddenly drawn to him like a magnet. I stare into his mesmerising grey eyes as I throw my arms around his neck once more. Tiny electrical pulses run through me, making me shiver from his touch. My body yearns to be near him, the man that saved me from that monster.

His eyes widen with desire as I reach up onto my tiptoes and pull him in closer. Our lips connect with hot passion as he urgently crushes his mouth against mine. In that moment, the world around us melts away. There is no one else; there is only Colt.

LITTLE WHITE LIES

I made Colt swear that he wouldn't tell the others what had happened. After initially pushing back and insisting that we should be honest, I highlighted that we didn't need any more distractions today, and ultimately there was nothing to be gained from telling the truth. It's done now and I survived; rescuing Joe is all that matters. In the next twelve hours, we will be far from this place and what happened with Bobby will be history. I also asked him to keep quiet about the kiss too. I have never in my life had that all-consuming, burning desire to be with someone, to have their lips urgently on mine and to feel their arms wrapped around my waist.

I'm not usually the kind of girl that kisses a guy they just met, but there's something about Colt that draws me in like a moth to a flame, and I know in my heart that he feels it too. Ironically, when we first met I genuinely thought that he didn't even like me, and then twelve hours later, we're kissing like our lives depend on it.

At the end of the day, there's no denying that Colt is gorgeous. His smouldering grey eyes, chiselled body and messy brown hair would make any girl swoon. Even though Suzie warned that he's a heartbreaker, in that moment last night, he saw me at my most vulnerable, and he didn't even flinch.

He initially seemed hurt by my request to remain quiet, but after I explained that I had to prioritise Joe and Tommy over any potential relationship, he wholeheartedly agreed. A small part of me also worries about Will and how he will react, but of course I didn't mention that to Colt.

Things between Will and I have seemed tense lately, but he has never actually made a move on me. At the end of the day, he's my best friend. I would do anything for him, and I know that he feels the same for me. I'm sure the only thing that he will be concerned with is that Colt is good to me.

We returned to the tent after I'd cleaned myself up and climbed back into our respective bunk beds, almost as though nothing had happened. I slid in beside Tommy and snuggled him tightly, trying to rid my mind of Bobby. But every time I close my eyes, all I can see is that monster leaning over me and tugging at my panties.

A part of me wonders if I will ever get over what he tried to do to me; I can't even imagine how I would feel right now if he had managed to succeed. Even though I scrubbed myself raw in a boiling hot shower following the assault, my skin still crawls from his repulsive touch. As a result, I quickly realised there's no chance that I will be sleeping anytime soon.

To keep my thoughts away from Bobby, and to stop myself from having some kind of breakdown, I try to focus my mind on the day ahead and specifically Tommy's medical. I refuse to let that wretched excuse for a human being break me. Today is the day that we rescue Joe and begin our journey to Alhena. I will not be broken.

At six sharp, Suzie jumps up from her bunk bed and begins to yell at the soldiers to get ready for training. Will springs out of bed in shock, running his hands through his messy sandy hair. Suzie smiles and chuckles at him softly.

"Sorry to wake you guys… and you don't need to train, Will!"

Rubbing his bleary eyes, he tries to brush it off. "I could do with going for a run this morning anyway."

As I force a smile at him, my jaw begins to throb, making me wince in pain. Sucking in a sharp breath, I bring my hand up and tentatively touch it. Will is instantly at my side in a heartbeat, examining my jaw, quickly followed by Colt. Will looks at Colt with a puzzled expression, clearly wondering why he cares so much, and then angles his body to almost block him from getting any closer.

"How did that happen?"

My heart thumps inside my chest as I search for an excuse. Trying to keep my voice even, I say, "Probably from the fight with the Infected."

Nodding his head, he cups my face. "Maybe get the doctor to check it over when Tommy has his medical."

I roll my eyes at him. "I'm fine. It's just a bruise – I'll live."

Will takes a step backwards, looking up and down my body. "When did you get changed? Weren't you wearing a shirt when you went to bed?"

My face blanches as I tug at the hem of Colt's t-shirt nervously. I open my mouth to try and justify the wardrobe change but come up empty. I stare at Colt with wide eyes, desperate for some help as I stumble over my words.

"I took it off because I was way too hot… and when I

got up to pee in the night, I just found this on the floor and put it on."

I cringe inside at my lame excuse, but it was the best idea I had.

Will looks at me suspiciously. "Well, you should've woken me up. I don't want you wandering around this place by yourself at night; there are all kinds of crazy people lurking around here. Take Bobby, for example – that guy is a psycho!"

My mind flashes back to Bobby sitting in the corner of the container as a manic grin stretched across his face. I quickly close my eyes, trying to shake the image from my mind as a wave of nausea whirls in the pit of my stomach. I suddenly grab the edge of the bunk bed for support, feeling like I might pass out. Colt instinctively reaches out to support me but then thinks better of it and just stares at me with a look of despair. Will places his hand firmly on my shoulder and lowers his voice.

"What's going on, are you sick?"

I force a smile again. "Stop fussing over me. I'm fine. It's probably just low blood sugar or something. Tommy and I will go grab something to eat. You should take this opportunity and train with Suzie."

Eyeing me curiously, he clearly doesn't believe me. I straighten my posture and stare at him earnestly. "Stop it, I'm fine, honestly!"

Nodding his head, he backs away and doesn't push it any further. He turns to Suzie as she laces her boots. "Is it okay if I train with you guys?"

Suzie grins at him. "Sure, but don't expect me to go easy on you!"

Thankfully the entire squad, including Will, run out of the tent and into the training field for exercise. As Colt walks past, he pauses momentarily with a pained expression etched into his face before disappearing outside. Exhaling loudly, I can't help but wonder how long I can keep up with the lies before I get found out.

I glance over my shoulder and notice that Tommy is sat on the edge of the bunk bed looking decidedly gloomy. His sad expression instantly pushes Bobby from the forefront of my mind. I sit next to him and wrap my arm around his shoulder.

"What's going on, are you okay?"

He shakes his head. "I'm so scared about my medical. What happens if they find out about me and then lock me away in some lab? What if they try and kill me?"

I pull his shoulder around so that I can look him in the eye. "Tommy, I can guarantee that will not happen because I won't let it happen, okay? You said it yourself last night, we are all going to be leaving this place as a family and that includes you as well as Joe."

He tries to smile, but his eyes remain sad. Leaning over, I kiss his cheek and then stand up in front of him.

"Let's go get some breakfast and get ready. The sooner we do this, the sooner we can get Joe and the sooner we can get the hell out of here. How does that sound?"

His eyes become brighter at the sound of food. "I'm starving!"

Ruffling his hair, I tease, "You're hungry? Surely not?"

Tommy and I throw on some clothes and head for the mess tent to grab some breakfast. As we walk across the training field, the rising sun is obscured by a blanket of murky clouds, making the atmosphere feel warm and oppressive.

Several squads are training relentlessly under the watchful eyes of their lieutenants, kicking up clouds of dust in the process. In the distance, I see Suzie standing over her team with her hands on her hips counting their push-ups at the top of her voice. Amazingly, Will is in the midst of the squad and appears to be keeping up with the pace.

With the mess tent now in view, my pulse quickens with anxiety at the thought of seeing Bobby. I pause momentarily near the entrance, feeling lightheaded and sweaty. Tommy stares at me, concerned, but I quickly brush it off by mentally pushing myself through it. The last thing I need is to have a full-blown panic attack in view of everyone in this compound.

Trying to steady myself, I take a deep breath and quickly step around the corner, to be confronted by a near empty tent with only a few soldiers dotted at random tables. Sighing with relief, I realise that Bobby is nowhere to be seen.

I shakily wipe away the beads of sweat on my forehead and push Tommy eagerly towards the food service. I quickly grab some fruit, bread and cheese and head for an empty table at the back, far away from any soldiers that could potentially listen to us. Even though Bobby is nowhere to be seen, I still can't help but feel on edge.

Biting my lip anxiously, I look down at my delicious plate of fresh fruit and suddenly feel nauseated. I pick up a shiny red apple, feeling the weight of it in my hand as a feeling of defiance begins to burn in my chest. I need my strength today, and I'll be damned if Bobby puts me off my food. Taking a huge bite into the apple, I let the juicy sharpness fill my mouth and focus on trying to swallow the damn thing without retching. To distract myself further, I speak between mouthfuls.

"Okay, so while we have the opportunity, let's chat through the medical." A look of determination spreads across Tommy's face as I continue, "Remember the story – you got into a fight at school and your back was scratched in the process. Otherwise, you have never been sick." He nods his head, and I reach out and hold his hand. "I'll do most of the talking, so don't worry too much."

Tommy frowns a little. "And what if they want to take samples, like blood?"

I stare at him earnestly. "You need to let them take it from you. I'll create some kind of diversion and switch the samples as we discussed last night." A grin spreads across my face as I quip, "As Joe would call it… the old switcheroo!"

Tommy can't help but smile at me in response. "I can't wait to have Joe back."

My heart twinges inside my chest. "Me too."

Tommy and I spend the rest of our breakfast trying to distract each other, which is a welcome relief from all the worries whirling around in my head. We talk about Joe and the journey to Alhena; at one point we even start to talk about Mum and Dad. We chat for so long that we even go for a second breakfast, which seems so alien to me. Suzie eventually arrives in the tent and walks over to our table, smiling at us sweetly.

"Are you guys ready?"

Tommy and I look at each other. "Is it nine already?"

She shakes her head. "Not quite. You have about forty minutes, but I thought you may want to freshen up, and maybe I could just give you guys a final briefing." She pauses before speaking and raises her eyebrows. "And we need to make sure that you are fully prepared for the medical."

I furrow my brow and open my mouth to question her, but she shakes her head subtly before I can ask. She gestures for us to follow her outside to make our final preparations.

When we arrive back at Suzie's tent, Colt and Will are standing awkwardly to one side. Will smiles as soon as he sees us approaching.

"Feeling better?"

Nodding my head, I look at Will and then pointedly at Colt. "I'm fine."

Colt seems to relax a little by my admission, whereas Suzie seems completely oblivious to the tension rising in the tent around her. Dashing forward, she hurriedly digs into the bottom of her trunk and pulls out a needle and syringe.

"Okay, I need a volunteer!"

She looks between Will and Colt, as I tentatively take a step forward.

"I'll do it. Tommy is my brother."

She shakes her head. "I don't know the first thing about blood, but I think it should be one of the boys just to be safe. I assume they will know if the sample is male or female, so it's not worth the risk."

I turn around to look at Will and Colt as they both answer at the same time: "I'll do it!"

Suzie shifts her weight impatiently. "I don't care who gives it, but we need to do it now before the squad come back from the showers."

Suzie points at Colt. "Private, you're up!"

Without hesitating, he walks towards Suzie and offers his arm.

"I hope you know what you're doing, Lieutenant?"

She shrugs her shoulders. "I don't have a clue, but how hard can it be?"

Colt visibly swallows as a smirk quivers at the corner of Will's mouth. "Man, how embarrassing would it be if you passed out right now?"

Suzie wraps a band around Colt's bicep as she glares at Will. "If you want, I can practice on you first?"

Will blanches a little at the thought of Suzie taking his blood, but shakes it off quickly to save face. Colt, on the other hand, stares at me intensely and seems unfazed by Will's taunting. He clenches his fist as Suzie steadily pushes the needle into his arm. Colt winces in pain as she pulls it back out again.

"Sorry, sweetheart, second time lucky!"

She slides the needle into his arm once more as Colt grits his teeth.

Tommy watches wide-eyed and whispers in my ear, "It's not going to hurt that much, is it?"

Trying to reassure him, I say, "Not in the slightest. The reason it's hurting Colt so much is that Suzie has no idea what she's doing. The doctor at the medical will have lots of experience with taking blood."

Suzie finally removes the needle from Colt's arm, having successfully taken a full vial of blood. She studies it curiously before shoving it into my hand.

"You might want to tuck this into your bra – they may search you when you enter the lab."

Without even pausing to look at it, I reach underneath

my shirt and tuck it inside the cup of my bra. Suddenly, the sound of footsteps can be heard approaching outside the tent. Suzie instantly lunges forwards and flings the syringe into the bottom of her trunk before approaching Tommy and me.

"Remember everything that I said, okay? Try to keep your head down and don't draw any unnecessary attention – and don't forget to steal a key card too!"

My heart skips a beat as the gravity of the situation sinks into the pit of my stomach. Staring at me with a grave expression, Suzie raises her chin.

"Don't screw it up. Joe's life depends on it."

Walking past us, she pulls back the entrance of the tent and gestures forwards. Exhaling loudly, I mumble to myself as we all head to the lab, "So… no pressure then."

DOWN THE RABBIT HOLE

We all arrive outside the entrance of the lab, waiting nervously to enter. A steep slope leads down to a circular sand-coloured door with two overwhelmingly bored soldiers stationed outside. Unless you specifically know where the lab is, you could almost walk straight past it; whoever designed the lab clearly intended for it to be a secret.

At ground level, there's no evidence that there is a lab of any sort, which means it must be fully underground. A chill runs down my spine as I look down at my feet and wonder how deep this underground complex goes. Tommy stands beside me with a look of sheer panic on his face. I reach down to try and hold his hand and realise that I'm shaking like a leaf. In contrast, Colt stands directly behind me and radiates a sense of calm. Placing his hand gently on my shoulder, he pulls me round to make eye contact with him.

"If I have learnt anything about you, it's that you can handle this."

With glistening eyes, he pulls me into a tight hug, crushing me against his solid chest. My body initially tenses from his touch, suddenly nervous at the public display of affection, but within seconds, my nerves are quickly replaced with an all-consuming desire to kiss him. Releasing me from the hug, he looks down at me and then delicately tucks an errant hair behind my ear.

"I'll see you soon."

I turn around, feeling a little giddy, to be confronted by a confused Will. Raising his eyebrows, he quickly shakes it off and opens his arms, pulling me into a tight hug too. He picks me up from the ground and spins me around, planting a firm kiss on my cheek.

"You got this! Give 'em hell!"

Suzie rolls her eyes beside us. "No, don't give them hell. Just get in and get out – safely."

She then walks down ahead of us and begins to chat to the soldiers currently on duty outside the entrance, probably confirming our arrival. Will reaches out, absentmindedly intertwining his fingers with mine, and begins to walk me down the slope towards the entrance. He drapes his other arm lazily over Tommy's shoulder, leaving Colt behind at the top.

Suzie introduces us to the soldiers on duty and speaks in a formal tone: "You need to follow Private Marshal. He will take you directly to the medical centre. I'll be here waiting for you when you're done."

I glance over my shoulder to see Colt standing at the top of the slope with his arms crossed over his chest. From the look of his expression, he seems relaxed and unfazed by Will's affection towards me. He continues to smile at me and nods his head once, silently sending a message of encouragement. I turn to the soldiers on guard duty.

"Okay, we're ready."

Private Marshal stares at me with the most bored face that I have ever seen. With a deadpan expression, he mumbles, "Please follow me."

He pushes down heavily on a rusty lever attached to the circular door and then pulls it sharply towards us. The sound of compressed air whistles loudly as it escapes from the seams. Standing to one side, he holds the door back and gestures for us to step through the threshold. I cast one final look to Suzie, Will and Colt stood at the top of the slope before quickly grabbing Tommy's hand and heading inside the lab entrance.

My heart pounds in my chest as we step through into a gloomy makeshift corridor. The female guard on duty remains stationed outside and forcefully closes the door behind us with a clunk. She looks through a small, dirty window with a blank expression and signals to Private Marshal before pulling the lever up sharply and locking us inside.

Not wasting any time, our escort turns on his heel and marches down the long dark corridor towards an ominous door at the far end. His boots clink on the rusty metal floor, as water drips down the wooden pillars supporting the uneven stone ceiling. The temperature is much cooler than the surface, and with the absence of any natural light, a feeling of unease creeps into my bones.

Private Marshal pulls back the heavy door to reveal a rickety caged elevator that looks as though riding it may result in us all plummeting to our deaths. Tommy walks stiffly beside me and whispers, "I don't like this."

As I stare into his frightened eyes, I swallow back my own fear and force a smile.

"You don't need to be scared. Everything will be okay, I promise."

The soldier pulls back the caged door with a rattle and

ushers us through impatiently. Leaning over me, he hits a large red button with his fist, making the elevator jolt to life. My stomach flips as we begin to make our speedy descent into darkness. As the elevator plummets at an unrelenting pace, I instantly regret that second breakfast. Grabbing onto the handrail for support, I swallow hard and hope that it ends soon.

I look up to see Tommy staring at me with wide eyes; he's clutching the hand rail so tightly that his knuckles are starting to turn white. Taking an unsteady step towards him, I quickly place my hand over his and subtly attempt to pry his fingers back without the soldier witnessing. The last thing we need is for Tommy to rip off the solid metal handrail before we even set foot in the medical centre. Fortunately, the elevator finally comes to a halt, making us all stumble in the process. Tommy releases his hand from the rail to reveal a slight dent in the metal. Given the current state of the rest of the elevator, I doubt that anyone will notice.

Private Marshal pulls back another solid metal door to reveal a bright white corridor with fluorescent lighting. The sheer luminance reflecting off the clinical walls instantly makes my eyes water. The sharp, angular contours running fluidly along the white metal walls give the lab an otherworldly appearance. Tommy and I hesitate near the elevator exit, feeling intimidated by this alien world. Our escort paces ahead and mumbles in a bored monotone voice, as though he's done this a hundred times before.

"You need to go into decontamination before you go into the lab."

Glancing at Tommy, I nervously step into the corridor, still trying to process the contrast between the gloomy, cave-like entrance near the surface to this blindingly bright hallway. As we begin to shuffle down the length of the corridor, I reach out and defensively wrap my arm around Tommy's shoulder, suddenly feeling completely out of my depth.

I have never in my life seen anything like this place and rather naïvely, I had no idea that places like this still existed. I guess that's the problem with living in an isolated compound in the middle of nowhere for your entire life.

Private Marshal presses a green button to confirm our arrival and then swipes his key card against an electric scanner. My eyes instantly light up at the sight of his card, making my mind whirl with all the possibilities of how to steal it. Sighing heavily, I realise I need to bide my time and not rush. This guy may be bored and hate his job, but I need to choose the perfect opportunity to steal the key without getting caught. He pushes open the seamless, heavy white door and gestures forward.

"Go through the door on your right. They are expecting you."

Before I can even respond, he shuts the door behind us, leaving us to fend for ourselves. Exhaling loudly, I puff out my cheeks, feeling a little exasperated. Tommy furrows his brow and then whips his head behind us and glares at a tiny security camera pointing directly at us. My heart sinks as I realise that stealing the key card just got more complicated. The sound of a female voice suddenly booms from somewhere unseen.

"Please enter through the door on your right."

I shakily grab Tommy's hand once more and head for decontamination. We slowly walk into a small room where one of the walls is made entirely of darkened glass. Taking a step forward, I tentatively place my palms on the glass and curiously peer through it, wondering what the hell is on the other side. My question is quickly answered, as a bright light suddenly flashes behind it, revealing a red-headed woman in a long white coat staring at us with a clipboard. She leans over and speaks through a microphone.

"I need you to strip down to your underwear and stand with your arms behind your head."

Tommy and I quickly look at each other. Placing my hand on my hips I begin to feel a little indignant at being ordered around without an explanation.

"Do you want to tell us exactly what's going on here?"

Setting her jaw firmly, the technician presses the microphone impatiently.

"As you have both been on the surface, you need to be completely sterilised of any potential contaminates that could compromise our research."

I shake my head at her. "Okay, fine. But can you tell us exactly how you're going to 'decontaminate' us?"

She gives me an icy glare. "Once you have removed your clothes and placed them in the plastic bag provided at your feet, you need to place the face masks over your mouth and nose. I will then spray you with a chemical that will completely decontaminate you both."

I give her a sarcastic smile. "Decontaminate us from what? We're not sick, and we haven't been around any Infected... not for at least twelve hours anyway."

Staring at me with an emotionless expression, she ignores my question. "Once you exit through the adjacent door, there's a box with some scrubs that you can wear while you are in the premises. Now please remove your clothes. I am extremely busy today."

Cursing under my breath, I angrily strip down to my underwear in two seconds flat, quickly followed by Tommy. I grab our face masks from the floor, passing one to Tommy and shoving the other one over my face.

Placing my hands firmly behind my head, I glare at this woman and ask, "Quick enough for you?"

The technician slams her hand on a button, making a light in the corner of the room flash red. An alarm blips three times as an automated voice booms over the tannoy speakers: "*Commencing decontamination.*"

I open my mouth to try and soothe an anxious Tommy, but the room suddenly fills with a noxious gas, making my eyes and nose burn. We both reflexively hold our breath to minimise the gas entering our lungs. I look over at Tommy and see that his eyes are red raw and streaming as he struggles to hold his breath.

Thankfully, after a few minutes the light in the corner suddenly switches off and is replaced by the sound of a roaring ventilation fan; my hair whips around my shoulders as the gas is sucked out of the vents in the ceiling almost as quickly as it appeared. We both breathe deeply and rub our stinging eyes as the door automatically opens beside us. I angrily step forwards to shout at the idiot technician behind the glass, but quickly realise that she is nowhere to be seen.

Feeling bewildered, I look at Tommy and place my hand on his back.

"Are you okay?"

He nods his head slowly. "Yeah, but that lady has issues."

A grin stretches across my face. "That's one way of putting it."

Leaving the 'gas chamber', we grab our light-blue scrubs and speedily get dressed before wandering out into another white corridor. As soon as we exit, we are met by a blond-haired soldier that is similar in age to Colt. He stares at us both with his kind blue eyes and offers a handshake, smiling at us.

"Good morning. My name is Lee. You must be Alyx and Tommy?"

Rubbing my sore eyes with the back of my hand, I look at him wearily. "That's us."

Taking a step towards us, he looks concerned. "Did they not give you any goggles to wear?"

"No, that red-haired asshole never mentioned anything about goggles."

"I'm so sorry about that. Jennifer has a bit of a reputation…"

Losing my patience, I say, "I can't say that I'm surprised. Without sounding rude, can you show us where we need to go, so we can get this over with?"

"I'll be escorting you today. Don't worry. I can assure you that Dr Al Bayati is very nice. If you would like to follow me, I'll take you straight to the medical centre."

Lee holds open a double door to reveal another long white corridor that is buzzing with activity. At the far end, the corridor flows into an open expanse with several doctors and technicians busily walking between labs. Others relax in seated areas – or as Lee calls them, 'pods' – drinking coffee and reading books.

Tall green trees line the inner walls and the domed

ceiling has a computer-generated video of a rolling clear blue sky, almost giving the illusion that we really are outside rather than deep beneath the earth's surface. Lee looks over his shoulder at us as he continues walking forward.

"This is the main atrium. You can access most areas of the lab from this point."

A million questions whirl around in my mind as I try to absorb every last detail of this place.

"When was the lab built? Surely it must have been created before the infection? Otherwise, where did all this infrastructure come from?"

Lee smiles at me eagerly. "Originally it was a government building long before the spread of infection; however, given the location, they decided to convert it into a research facility. As it's underground, it was relatively easy for the research to continue post-infection. However, it hasn't been without its issues. That's why there's a military base on the surface protecting this place."

I open my mouth to question Lee further on these 'issues' but he paces ahead and then stops abruptly, pointing to a holographic image projected on the white wall.

"Take a look at this."

As I lean forward to study it in more detail, an automated voice sounds: "*Please confirm destination.*" My eyes widen as the map suddenly begins to glow and rotate, colour-coding each branch of the lab complex. Reaching up instinctively, I begin to trace my fingers over the various destinations while simultaneously attempting to memorise it for future reference. Lee turns and grins at me.

"Pretty cool, huh?"

Staring at him open-mouthed, I say, "This is insane!"

He smiles at me and then begins to usher me forwards once more. "The medical centre is on the other side of the atrium."

Putting my curiosity to one side, I quickly follow Lee across the atrium in a daze and walk through a quiet corridor with a large sign directing us to the medical centre. Lee approaches a young, pretty girl with black-framed glasses sitting behind a desk.

She smiles at us politely and says, "Please take a seat. Dr Al Bayati will be with you in a moment."

I look over at Tommy who is looking decidedly pale with a tinge of redness still rimmed around his eyes. I take his hand gently and encourage him to sit down next to me and wait for the doctor to arrive. As I take a deep breath and try to focus on the task ahead, I notice several black and white photos are hung on a wall in front of us. From the age of the photos, I assume they were probably taken before the spread of the infection.

As I lean forward to have a closer look, there's one photo in the centre that grabs my attention: two young men in lab coats, probably in their early twenties, smiling goofily at the camera. While the photo in itself is quite ordinary, one of the men reminds me of someone, but I can't quite remember who.

I stand up and lean closer to study the photo in more detail as the door suddenly opens. A deeply tanned man with jet-black hair steps out. From the look of his face, I would guess that he is in his early sixties.

He smiles at us, trying to ease the tension and offers his hand. "Hi, I'm Dr Asliraf Al Bayati, but everyone calls me Al. You must be Alyx and Tommy."

Smiling at him politely, I say, "Hello, Al, nice to meet you."

He points to the photo that I was staring at. "The days of college before all this madness started."

I raise my eyebrows at him. "That's you?"

"I was young once, you know!" he retorts.

I point to the other man in the photo. "And who's that in the photo with you?"

His smile falls from his face as a look of sorrow creeps into his eyes.

"That's my best friend, Art."

Furrowing my brow, I realise that I don't know anyone called Art, so I question him further. "Art? That's an unusual name."

He sighs heavily. "It's short for Arthur. He died around twelve years ago. We studied medicine together."

Cogs begin to slowly turn in my mind as I try to maintain a blank expression.

"I'm sorry to hear that. What was Arthur's surname? His face reminds me of someone I once knew."

He points to the photo once more with a look of nostalgia on his face.

"Dunlop… his name was Arthur Dunlop."

THE OLD SWITCHEROO

My mind whirls as I try to process Al's words. The man in the photo is Arthur Dunlop, the same man that was experimenting on the Infected that resulted in Tommy almost dying and gaining new unexplainable and damn right scary 'abilities'. The same man that may or may not have created the cure for the infection in the process and who is still very much alive back home in Merope.

My palms become sweaty as I desperately try to keep my expression nonchalant; maybe he knows that Arthur is still alive, and he's trying to catch me out? Or maybe he genuinely thinks that he's dead. Either way, I can't trust him until I have more answers. Clearing my throat a little, I force a sympathetic smile across my face.

"Sorry to hear that your friend passed away."

He nods his head. "It was all a bit of a tragedy to be honest. He was a brilliant man with huge potential."

Holding back the door, he gestures into his room. "Please come through, and we can get started."

I nervously look over at Tommy; he has somehow managed to become even more pale than he was before. Rubbing his back, I guide him forwards and cautiously walk into Al's office. The room is much like the rest of the lab:

white, clinical and filled with technology that completely blows my mind.

It's clear from the way that the room is maintained that Al is extremely organised; all of his books are displayed neatly in alphabetical order, and the medicines are labelled clearly and locked behind immaculate glass cabinets. There's little evidence of any personal effects. The only remotely personal belonging that I can see is a white chipped coffee mug that has a faded I HEART SPREADSHEETS on the side.

Tommy walks stiffly over to a long black leather trolley in the corner and perches nervously on the edge, while Al sits in front of his computer and begins to type. He smiles at Tommy warmly, clearly noticing the look of fear etched into his face.

"It's okay, Tommy. You have absolutely nothing to worry about. This is all completely routine so just try to stay relaxed."

Tommy stares at Al wide-eyed and nods his head once as Al continues, "Okay, so my associates inform me that during your initial body search to enter the compound, they saw a scratch on your back? Is that correct?"

Unable to maintain eye contact, Tommy lowers his gaze and begins to swing his feet. "Yeah, I was at school and got into a fight with this other kid… and he scratched me."

Al nods his head as he continues to type on his computer. "I see… Would you mind if I have a look?"

Tommy slowly tugs at the hem of his shirt and then pulls it over his head. Standing up from his desk, Al steps over to have a closer look and furrows his brow.

"Huh, that must have been quite a fight to leave scratch marks like that. I've seen similar wounds from wild animals.

From the colouration of the scars, I'm guessing this happened quite some time ago?"

Tommy simply nods his head without speaking, while Al raises his eyebrows and returns to his desk to type into his computer. It's clear from his expression that he doesn't believe that Tommy was scratched by another kid at school, but to be honest, anyone with half a brain cell can see that he wasn't.

However, as I study his body language, Al generally seems relaxed and unfazed because to most people Tommy isn't showing any traditional signs of infection. Stopping momentarily, Al looks up from his computer screen and smiles politely.

"Okay, well, given that you are clearly not exhibiting any other symptoms associated with virus N3-vR2, whether you were scratched by another child or by a bear for that matter, I am happy to issue clearance for you to remain in Panama."

I sigh with relief and begin to stand. "That's great. Thanks so much for seeing us today."

Al holds up his hand.

"We are not quite finished here yet. Even though Tommy has clearance to stay, I still need to proceed with a few routine tests to complete the medical. Nothing to be worried about. It's just standard procedure."

I exhale loudly, knowing it was too good to be true. I slump back down in my seat as Al grabs his stethoscope. He pulls his seat round in front of Tommy and places the silver disc on his chest, directly next to his heart. A look of concentration spreads across his face as he looks up at Tommy.

"Your heart sounds normal, which is good, but you do have bradycardia. Do you exercise much?"

Leaning forward in my seat nervously, I start to feel a little shaky. This is the part when things could go terribly wrong, and there's nothing that I can do to stop it. Exhaling quietly, I try to keep my voice even.

"What's bradycardia exactly?"

He turns around to address me. "Tommy has an abnormally slow heartbeat, which is usually associated with those that exercise everyday – like athletes for example."

Trying to keep my expression blank, the lie easily forms at my lips. "Joe makes us train every day in case there is a breach in the village. Survival of the fittest, right?"

Nodding his head, he smiles. "Indeed, and of course, any form of exercise is good."

Tommy wipes his forehead with the back of his hand nervously, as Al pulls out a small contraption from his lab coat.

"I'm just going to take your temperature now. This part here goes inside your ear."

Leaning forward, he gently places the thermometer in Tommy's ear and studies the gauge. Furrowing his brow, a look of puzzlement spreads across his face.

"Your temperature is a little low for your age. Some children can have lower than average temperature, but at your age it's far less common. Have you had a cold or flu recently?"

Tommy lowers his gaze and shakes his head meekly. "No, I'm fine."

Al leans forward to meet his gaze and stares at him earnestly. "I'm not here to catch you out. Just because you have had a cold doesn't mean that you are infected. I'm here to help you."

Tommy glares at him as a look of irritation flashes across his face. Speaking more assertively now, he says, "I'm not sick, okay?"

Al narrows his eyes and raises his chin. "Okay, well, if you start to feel unwell, let me know, and I'll be more than happy to take another look at you."

As tension begins to rise in the room, I suddenly panic that Tommy may lash out at the doctor. Quickly interjecting, I try to dissipate the situation.

"He's probably just a little run down. We've been through a lot in the last few days, especially with Joe in jail. I'll make sure that he gets plenty of rest and some good food in his belly."

Al returns to his desk again to write more notes into his computer.

"That sounds reasonable. Depending on how long you are planning on staying, I would suggest that you come down for a check-up in a day or so. Just to be safe."

I force a smile. "Thanks, but I don't think that will be necessary. We intend to leave as soon as possible. Probably tomorrow morning, maybe even tonight."

Nodding his head, Al spins around in his chair and pulls out a needle and syringe from a drawer, placing them directly into a metal dish. As soon as he puts on some blue latex gloves, I subtly scan the room for any evidence of security cameras, and fortunately I can't see any. Walking over to Tommy, he wraps a tourniquet around his bicep and then pulls his arm out flat.

"Okay, so I'm going to take a blood sample now. You'll

feel a sharp little scratch. Just try to stay relaxed, and it will be over soon."

Tommy clenches his fist and grits his teeth as my mind spins into overdrive – time for the old switcheroo.

Jumping to my feet I blurt out, "You don't mind if I take a look around, do you? I can't stand the sight of blood!"

Without looking at me, Al mumbles, "Sure, just try not to touch anything."

I casually walk around the room and feign interest in the various machines stationed on the work surfaces while I search for my diversion. Leaning forward, I begin to fiddle with one of the machines.

"What does this one do here?"

Al maintains focus on the needle in Tommy's arm.

"Please don't touch, Alyx. Everything in this room is invaluable. I'll show you once I'm finished."

Ignoring him, I walk over to another machine, trying to keep him distracted.

"Where do you get all this cool stuff from? Back home in Merope our medical facilities consisted of a bed, herbal medicine and a sick bucket."

Becoming agitated from fiddling with his precious machines, Al quickly finishes taking Tommy's blood and places the sample in the metal tray. He walks over to where I am standing, puts the tray on the counter beside me and points to the machine that I am investigating.

"Most of the machines were here before the spread of the infection… and that is an autoclave. It's a steriliser."

I smile at him enthusiastically. "Cool, so what about this one…"

Before I finish my sentence, I gesture wildly with my left

hand and deliberately knock over a glass beaker, smashing it onto the floor. I bring my hands up to my face pretending to be shocked.

"Oh, my goodness I'm so sorry! I'm so damn clumsy. Here let me help!"

I kneel down and begin to grab the sharp glass in my hands as Al springs into action.

"No, don't do that. You'll cut yourself. I'll grab a broom."

He paces to the other side of the room as I continue to gush with apologies. As soon as his back is turned, I reach inside my bra, grab Colt's blood sample and replace it with Tommy's. With the samples successfully switched, I notice Tommy exhale with relief as he shakily runs his hands through his hair. Al scoops up the shattered glass, pours it into a bin and then walks over to Tommy.

"You feel okay after the blood test?"

Tommy smiles for the first time today. "I feel good actually."

I can't help but smirk as Al picks up Colt's blood sample and writes Tommy's name on it – part one of this crazy mission is officially completed. Al quickly offers his hand out to Tommy.

"Okay, we're done here. As far as I'm concerned you're good to go, but if you start to feel poorly, please feel free to drop by before you leave."

Tommy shakes his hand and thanks him before jumping to his feet. Al turns round as I hold my hands up apologetically.

"Al, I am so sorry again. Thank you for all your help."

Guiding us towards the door, he's clearly eager for us to

leave before we damage anything else. "No harm done. It's been a pleasure meeting you both."

As soon as we walk out into the corridor, Lee stands up to greet us with his key card dangling from his right pocket.

"All done?"

Sighing with relief, I say, "Yep, all done!"

As I stare into his round, kind blue eyes, a part of me feels guilty that I have to steal his key card from him, but unfortunately, he is the perfect target: overly nice, eager to please and no doubt easy to manipulate too. At the end of the day, Joe's life depends on that key card. I just hope that he doesn't get into too much trouble for 'losing' his card.

I smile at him sweetly as we follow him out of the medical centre and head back in the direction of the atrium. Lee chats as he guides us back through, but I can't focus on anything that he is saying. My eyes dart around us, searching for cameras and any potential witnesses to my crime. I only have one shot at getting this right; if I screw it up, not only do I run the risk of getting caught, but it could mean that Joe will die.

My mouth becomes dry as I close the distance between me and Lee, walking almost shoulder to shoulder. Thankfully the atrium is much quieter this time. Most of the people seem to have disappeared, probably heading to their various jobs for the day. My mind races ahead, thinking back to our journey from the elevator: did Lee use his key card at any point? I can't remember him using it. The only person that I've seen using a key card so far is the marvellous Private Marshal.

Tuning back into the conversation, I notice that Lee starts to chuckle beside me, so I fake a laugh and smile at him, placing my hand gently on his lower back. He initially seems surprised by my touch, but small gestures like this can make all the difference when it comes to actually stealing his card. Reaching out, I place my hand on his elbow to grab his attention.

"So, will you be escorting us back up to the surface? Or will it be the overly enthusiastic Private Marshal?"

He rolls his eyes at me. "Ignore him, he hates doing this. I prefer working down here to up on the surface. The people are much nicer, the environment is better…"

As we round the corner and approach the door leading through to the 'gas chamber', I continue nodding at him and seemingly give him my undivided attention.

"Unfortunately, though, I won't be your guide to the surface… Private Miserable will meet you on the other side of the decontamination unit. But on the plus side, Miss Moody, aka Jennifer, won't spray you again. You can just get dressed and head up into the elevator. Your clothes will be where you left them."

I laugh at him heartily. "What's that you were saying? People are nicer down here?"

Lee grins at my lame joke and stares into my eyes awkwardly, almost as though he wants to say something to me but he's not sure how to say it. Ever the gentleman, he holds his hand out firmly in front of us as I smile at him encouragingly.

"It was great to meet you both. Hopefully I can see you again before you leave?"

With his breath caught in this throat, he scans my face for any mutual feelings as my heart pangs with guilt.

Closing the distance between us, I say, "That would be great!"

Catching him off guard, I ignore his offer for a handshake and open my arms, pulling him towards me into a tight, affectionate hug. He initially tenses at my touch but then pulls back and stares at me nervously with flushed cheeks. Stumbling over his words, he desperately tries to sound casual.

"Well that's great. I finish my shift around seven, so maybe we can hang out then?"

As I smile at him enthusiastically, I can't help but feel like a jerk. If all goes to plan, by seven o'clock this evening, we should be on our way to Alhena.

"Sure, I'll probably be in the mess tent or something, so come find me."

With my hand firmly in my pocket, Tommy and I turn around and walk through the door into the decontamination unit, leaving a love-struck Lee behind us. As soon as the door closes, I lean forwards and rest my hands on my knees as relief washes over me like a tidal wave. I can't believe I managed to pull this off without getting caught. I also can't quite believe how easy it was to manipulate Lee.

Tommy strips off his clothes speedily, suddenly reminding me that it's not over until we get the hell out of here. Being careful to keep the key card and Tommy's blood sample hidden, I put on Colt's t-shirt, which brings back memories from the moment that he took it off.

Biting my bottom lip, a smile quivers at the corner of my mouth as images of his kiss come flooding back into the forefront of my mind. I can't wait to celebrate our success with everyone. Hopefully my celebration also involves some kind of secret making-out session with Colt.

With my heart in my throat, we race back through the

opposing door to be met by Private Miserable. As we walk towards the elevator, for the first time in days I start to feel hopeful. Today we managed to successfully sneak Tommy through a medical without raising suspicion and steal a key card. All we need to do now is save Joe and get to Alhena. How hard could that be?

WHEN HOPE FADES

Private Marshal signals to the female soldier on guard duty through the small, dirty window in the circular door. Disappearing momentarily, she pushes down on the rusty lever with a loud clunk, pulling the door sharply towards her. As soon as the door begins to swing wide open, the dim, stagnant corridor is suddenly filled with a welcome rush of fresh air.

The soldier holds back the door as Tommy tentatively steps across the threshold into the glaring mid-morning sun. Following closely behind, I take a deep breath as a feeling of overwhelming relief floods through me. We succeeded in our mission: the blood samples were switched and a key card secured, amazingly without getting caught in the process.

Suzie is waiting at the top of the slope with her arms folded firmly over her chest. My heart sinks when I realise that Colt and Will are nowhere to be seen. Feeling a little panicked, I walk speedily up the slope to greet her, closely followed by Tommy.

"Where are they? What's happened?"

Smiling at me sweetly, she holds her hands up. "Everything is fine. They are both okay. Given that we are short on time and have a lot to do, I've been keeping the boys busy. I'll explain on the walk back."

Suzie thanks the soldiers on guard duty and begins to walk in the direction of her tent. The compound has sprung into life since our adventure in the labs earlier this morning. More soldiers have gathered on the walls for patrol and another group unload supplies from a shipping container into a vehicle.

As I stare at them curiously, Suzie confirms, "Prepping for recon."

I raise my eyebrow. I have no idea what recon is.

"It's short for reconnaissance. Once a fortnight a group will go out to gather supplies, bring down numbers of Infected and generally report back on anything that is happening outside these damn walls."

My chest begins to tighten. I realise that this may not be good for us in terms of trying to escape – they have a team preparing to leave for a long journey outside the compound.

Noticing my anxiety, Suzie says, "They are due to leave tomorrow." She smiles at me mischievously as she continues, "But don't worry. I have a feeling that the recon vehicles are going to have 'mechanical issues' between now and when they are due to leave…"

Grinning at her, I can't help but be amazed by Suzie. She has thought of everything. She holds back the entrance to her tent.

"Okay, you two go first, and then I'll give you an update on the boys and what we've been doing."

I give Tommy a sideways glance as he blurts, "We smashed it. Blood sample switched and key card stolen!"

Suzie seems surprised by Tommy's overwhelming

enthusiasm. This is the first glimpse that we've had of the 'old Tommy' since he was scratched. Smiling at us, Suzie slaps us on the back.

"I never doubted you guys, not even for a moment. Great job!"

Tommy beams at me, wrapping his arm around my back. "It was all Alyx. She was amazing!"

I present Lee's key card and then grab Tommy's blood sample out of my bra.

"We were due some good fortune after everything that has happened to us. As Tommy said, blood samples were switched, nothing major came out of the medical that made the doctor too suspicious, and I managed to secure the key card... and a date apparently."

At that moment, Will suddenly walks through the entrance of the tent.

"Who said you were allowed to date anyone?"

Grinning at me, he pulls me into a tight hug and then ruffles Tommy's hair. Looking up at Will, I can't help but feel a little defensive.

"I can date whoever I want."

Staring at me curiously, he quips, "See, that's what you think. You don't need anyone else, especially when you already have someone as awesome as me in your life!"

Suzie rolls her eyes beside us. "That's great, guys, really, but we have a million things to do right now, so can we focus please?"

Shifting my weight, I fold my arms across my chest defensively. Will and I have been inseparable for as long as I can remember. Maybe he won't be as okay with the idea of me and Colt as I initially thought. Either way, Suzie is right.

We have so many more important things to focus on right now than my complicated love life.

Suzie takes Tommy's blood sample, rolls it under her bunk bed and then smashes it with her boot. "Now that's taken care of, we can focus on getting the hell out of here and rescuing Joe. Okay, so Colt is currently on a fake mission outside the walls in a vehicle. He's going to leave it near to the air vent exit, so as soon as we escape through the tunnel, we can jump in a vehicle and head for Alhena."

My heart pounds inside my chest with concern. "He's outside the walls by himself? How far is the air vent? Is he coming back on foot?"

Suzie sets her jaw firmly. "It's not an ideal situation, but the reality is that we won't get far without a vehicle. He had to go by himself because we can't risk anyone else being involved. At the end of the day, Colt has trained for this. He can handle it."

Will interjects, "Do you guys usually go on solo missions like this? Won't it look suspicious when Colt doesn't come back in a vehicle?"

Suzie sighs heavily. "Going on a solo mission is generally against protocol, but it does happen on exceptional occasions. He's going to feign mechanical problems, call it in, and then someone will be sent to pick him up. It will be fine. Don't worry."

I'm sure Suzie is right. Colt has trained for this but the bleak reality is that he may have to deal with a horde of Infected on his own, and no matter how much he has trained, in that scenario his chances of survival are slim. The thought makes my stomach flip as Suzie looks to Will.

"How did you get on with the rations?"

Will holds up two rucksacks stuffed with food. "I explained to the guys down at the mess tent that Alyx, Tommy and I would be leaving shortly after the trial and would need provisions. They didn't even question it. They said we need to go over to munitions, where we can get our swords back and a couple of pistols if we're lucky… but only when we're ready to leave and not a moment before."

Suzie nods her head with a solemn expression.

"Don't worry. I will sort out the guns and stash them ready for you when the trial finishes. If all goes to plan, we will only be using them on the Infected on our journey to Alhena anyway, but should the worst happen, we may need them sooner."

As the gravity of the situation begins to sink in, I can't comprehend how difficult this must be for Colt and Suzie; potentially there could be casualties today as a result of saving Joe and helping Tommy get to Alhena. Those casualties would be men and women who have trained alongside Colt and Suzie; some of them may even be considered friends. The surge of hope that I was feeling after the success from the medical is quickly fading and is now being replaced by fear and dread. Suzie runs her hand through her short blonde hair nervously and clears her throat.

"Okay, so we don't have long before the trial. You guys need to get yourselves cleaned up and get the bags packed ready to go. Split the food and water evenly between the bags, get another change of clothes… oh, and I have some survival packs in my trunk at the end of my bed. I have a few errands to run, so I'll meet you guys back here an hour before the trial?"

As we nod our heads, Suzie swiftly exits, leaving us alone

in the tent to prepare the bags. Feeling a little agitated, I stride over to Suzie's bunk bed and begin to dig through her belongings in her trunk. Will stands behind me.

"Everything okay? You seem a little tense."

Spinning around to confront him, I say, "Of course I am, aren't you? If we screw this up Joe dies… and if by some miracle we manage to succeed, people are going to die – men and women who are here to just do their jobs are going to die so we can save Joe!"

He takes a step towards me. "I bet every soldier in this compound would do the same thing for their family in a heartbeat… and besides, this is so much bigger than just saving Joe! Tommy could be the cure, and these men and women die every day trying to stop it from spreading. Yes, there's a risk that people may die today, but think of all the other millions of people we could save?"

Lowering my gaze, a single tear trickles down my cheek. "We don't know that. What if he isn't the cure? What if it's all for nothing?"

Will delicately lifts my chin to make eye contact. "I don't know about you, but I would rather die trying with even the smallest hope that we have the cure than to save a few soldiers who are willing to die for the same cause anyway."

Will slowly leans down, closing the distance between us, and gently kisses me on the forehead. "Don't give up on hope."

Releasing me from the hug, he stares at me intensely with his twinkling green eyes.

"Now let's get the bags ready and get the hell out of here."

As a feeling of defiance begins to spread inside my chest,

Tommy stands to one side with a smile quivering at the corner of his mouth.

"I don't know if I am the cure or not, but just think – me being a dumbass could actually save the world!"

Grinning at him, both Will and I burst out laughing. I stride over to Tommy and pull him into a tight hug.

"My dumbass brother saves the world – who would have thought it!"

Will, Tommy and I spend the next hour packing the bags to get ready for our departure this evening. A part of me is excited to leave this place and to be back outside in the depths of the forest, even with the prospect of fighting more Infected. Most importantly, I can't wait to see Joe; I think this may be one of the longest times that I have been away from him, since the days when he would leave Merope during the raids. I hope with all my heart that he has been treated well and has had a better experience than I have in this wretched place.

With the bags prepped, we begin to walk over to the shower block to get ourselves cleaned up before the trial. However much I hate this place, they have good showers, and I am going to take full advantage; after all, it will be a very long time before I have the opportunity to shower again. As we stroll around the corner to the shower block, we are met by Colt who is covered in black congealed blood from head to toe. My mouth falls open at the sight of him.

"What happened to you?"

He shrugs his shoulders. "Just had a small run-in with a few Infected on the way back. No big deal."

Running up to him, I wrap my arms around his neck

and resist the urge to press my soft lips into his. He chuckles softly in my ear.

"I'm covering you in blood."

Pulling back, I stare up at his steely grey eyes. "I don't care. Are you hurt?"

Looking down smiling, he says, "I'm fine. How about you? Everything go as planned?"

Will walks up next to us and nods his head at Colt. "Got into a bit of trouble?"

Prying his eyes away from me, Colt looks at Will. "Nothing I couldn't handle."

Will slaps Colt on the shoulder before walking into the shower block with an edge of sarcasm in his voice.

"Good to have you back, buddy!"

Tommy looks at me knowingly and quickly follows Will, leaving me and Colt alone outside.

Leaning down to me, he speaks in a gravelly voice, "Are you okay?"

"Yep, all went to plan, although you may have some competition on your hands…"

"Oh, is that so?" he says, raising his eyebrow.

"Not sure if you know him, but there's this guy called Lee, and he is so sweet but…" Leaning closer, I whisper, "He no longer has a key card."

Puffing his cheeks out, Colt smiles at me lazily. "Big blue eyes, blond hair? Looks like he couldn't hurt a fly Lee? To be honest, I think most guys would struggle to resist you, Alyx. Did you let the poor guy down gently at least?"

Looking up at him through my eyelashes, I say, "No, I'm meeting him at seven for a date actually."

Colt gives me a withering look. "You weren't joking

when you said I had competition on my hands, were you? I think I ought to do something about that right now!"

Grinning at me, Colt takes my hand and drags me around the corner towards a tight alleyway between two shipping containers, stopping abruptly at the sight of Suzie. Seeing us both hand in hand, she glares at Colt angrily.

"What's going on here, Private?"

Dropping my hand quickly, he takes a deep breath and chooses his words carefully.

"Suzie, please let me explain…"

Tilting her head to one side, she says, "Thanks, but I don't think you need to. I think it's pretty obvious what's happening or what was about to happen."

She whips her head around to glare at me. "What did I say to you? How can you guys even think about doing that with everything that's going on around you?"

My cheeks flush bright red with embarrassment. "We weren't going to—"

"I don't want to hear it… Alyx, just think about what you're doing here, okay. Get in the goddamn showers. Separately."

She storms off, shaking her head, before we can even explain. Colt turns to me and sighs heavily.

"Sorry, that was my fault."

Setting my jaw firmly, all the worries from earlier come flooding back with a vengeance. Men and women could die today, hell we could all die today, and here I am running around with Colt for secret making-out sessions. I take a step away from him, feeling ashamed of myself.

"She's right. We can't be sneaking around. We need to focus on Joe and getting out of here in one piece. I'm sorry. I can't do this right now. There's just too much at stake."

Colt looks visibly wounded by my words and bows his head. As I begin to walk away in the direction of the shower block, he calls out, "Whatever Suzie has told you about me, I'm not that guy anymore. I care about you, Alyx, and I hope you can give me a chance to prove myself."

A lump quivers in my throat, making my mouth feel dry. A part of me knows that Colt cares about me deeply. I can see it when he stares into my eyes. But right now, I don't have time to worry if Colt will break my heart or even if any potential relationship may upset Will. The trial is only a few hours away. I need to focus all my thoughts on Joe and surviving the next twenty-four hours.

Turning around to face Colt momentarily, I see the sincerity in his glistening grey eyes as I confirm, "I hope so too."

Turning my back on him, I trace my hands through my tangled hair, feeling emotionally drained, before heading into the showers without looking back.

JUDGE, JURY AND EXECUTIONER

The run-up to the trial races by in a blur. After we cleaned ourselves up and checked the bags again, Suzie met us at her tent for a final briefing. Colt stood to one side, appearing to be sullen and thoughtful throughout the briefing, making eye contact with me occasionally but overall keeping his distance. Will and Tommy stood directly beside me, soaking up every last detail of Suzie's instructions.

Despite how angry she was earlier with Colt and me, Suzie launched into full military mode and was back to her usual self. She went over the plan tirelessly in granular detail, so that there were no doubts on where we should be and what we should expect. The vehicle is waiting for us near the vent, the guns are hidden, Suzie and Colt have tampered with most of the vehicles inside Panama to stop anyone immediately following us, and we have enough rations to last us a few days. All we have to do now is break Joe out of prison using Lee's key card and escape undetected. I really wish it was as easy as it sounds.

The tension is palpable as we stand outside the only brick building in the whole of Panama and wait for Joe to arrive. The chapel has been turned into a makeshift courtroom as several senior officers arrive to witness the proceedings. I can't help but fidget as an overwhelming sense of anxiety gnaws deep inside the pit of my stomach. I quickly cross my arms over my chest to stop myself from shaking. Noticing my expression, Will wraps his arm around my waist as we continue to wait in agitated silence.

Colt and Suzie stand to attention directly outside the entrance on guard duty, cradling M16s and seemingly ignoring the three of us. When Suzie's radio suddenly sparks into life, she tilts her head to one side and listens to the instructions before gently nodding her head in our direction. He must only be moments away now.

Tommy nervously takes a step forward, clearly hearing Joe approach before the rest of us. With my heart in my throat, I hold my breath with anticipation and wait for Joe to appear. I automatically reach down and intertwine Will's calloused fingers with mine, taking comfort in the familiarity of his strong hands.

The soldiers guarding Joe obscure him from view as they begin to walk around the corner. Unable to wait a second longer, I run towards him with tear-stained eyes to be confronted by a group of burly male soldiers aiming their guns at me.

Skidding to a halt, I angrily shout at the men, "Let me see him!"

Joe pushes the soldiers to one side and leans forward between them, smiling at the sight of me. His brown hair is unkempt, and he has dark circles under his eyes from lack of sleep, but otherwise he looks unharmed.

"Hey, kiddo!"

Smiling at him, tears begin to flow down my face. "I missed you so much."

Joe's eyes glisten as he lowers his gaze. "Are you and your brother okay?"

I force a smile and try to hide the look of pain in my eyes. "We're absolutely fine."

The soldiers guarding Joe become impatient. "Ma'am, please step aside."

Gritting my teeth, I reluctantly step back and watch Joe walk into the chapel with his arms and legs shackled. The all-too-familiar anger bubbles inside my chest at the injustice of it all. How could they punish a man for loving his family too much? How could they sentence a man to death who refused to let two innocent children die?

The general suddenly appears from around the corner and paces towards the chapel with purpose. He walks past speedily without even so much as glancing in our direction.

Unable to hold my tongue, I blurt, "Nice to see you too, Sinter."

He stops in the doorway of the chapel and slowly turns around to face me. With my hands firmly planted on my hips, I continue, "Nice day to execute an innocent man, don't you think?"

He doesn't dignify me with a response but simply whispers something in Suzie's ear before disappearing inside. With the general now out of view, Suzie paces towards me and grabs me by the elbow.

"Don't be pulling stuff like that! I've now got to keep a close eye on you throughout the proceedings. If you cause any more trouble, the general has given me strict instructions to arrest you, Alyx."

I set my jaw firmly. "The guy is an asshole!"

Suzie gives me a measured look.

"Be that as it may, if this whole thing is going to work we need you here, not in a prison cell. Just keep your head down, okay? It won't take long." She gestures forward. "Let's get this over with."

As I look at the ominous redbrick chapel nestled in a sea of shipping containers and khaki-green tents, the sky above looks gloomy and overcast, a true reflection of the sense of foreboding creeping into the centre of my bones. Tommy looks at me wide-eyed with an expression of fear and anxiety etched into his face. Holding out my hand, he clasps it tightly as we steadily make our way into Joe's trial.

The inside of the chapel needs desperate attention. The white walls have peeled over time, revealing glimpses of the red bricks from the outside of the building. Two long cracks flow along the towering walls like streaks of lightning and a large wooden cross hangs precariously from the rafters.

At the front of the chapel, the general stands stoically behind a lectern in an immaculate military uniform with an array of medals hanging proudly on his lapel, while Joe sits on a bench in the front row surrounded by guards with his head held high. Suzie motions Will, Tommy and me to a bench in the back row then she pulls the ancient wooden doors shut behind us. As soon as we are seated, Suzie quietly walks to the front and takes a seat in the second row while Colt remains stationed next to the doors. Raising his angular chin, General Sinter narrows his focus on Joe and clears his throat before addressing the room.

"Good afternoon and thank you for your attendance at such short notice. Today is the trial for Lieutenant Joseph Hudson for deserting his position during May 2042. This trial is the first of its kind here in Panama, hence the location in the compound's questionable chapel.

"The trial will begin by Lieutenant Hudson providing his testimony. I will then call upon Lieutenant Suzanne Morgan as a witness to the stand, then a jury consisting of myself and my fellow officers will deliberate and provide the verdict. Does anyone have any questions on today's proceedings?"

General Sinter focuses his attention directly on me, almost as though he is goading me into responding. However much I want to jump to my feet and give this asshole a piece of my mind, Suzie's words resonate in my head. Gritting my teeth, I subtly shake my head as a smirk quivers at the corner of Sinter's mouth.

"Lieutenant Hudson, please stand and state how you plead?"

Joe slowly stands from the bench to address General Sinter. Even though I can only see the back of his head, I know only too well the expression that he has on his face: one of defiance, self-belief and determination.

Without even pausing to consider his words, he says, "Guilty."

A part of me expected that Joe would plead guilty, but it still didn't stop me from gasping. In my mind, Joe is innocent and always will be. The general nods his head in approval.

"Okay, good. This won't take long then. Please take my place here and state your case."

The chains around his ankles clink with every movement as he shuffles towards the lectern. A soldier accompanies him and stands directly behind. Joe sets his jaw firmly and speaks directly to the general with an air of resolve.

"My name is Joseph Hudson, and I plead guilty for deserting my position as a lieutenant in the 52nd Infantry Division of Alhena on May 22nd 2042."

Joe then proceeds to recount the entire story of the day that he rescued us. Even though between us we have retold this story a hundred times, the rawness of the details never fades. As I get older, I have to try and fill my mind with other memories of my parents: the bedtime stories, picking strawberries for the first time with my mum. Otherwise, I fear that one day the only memory that I will have will be the look of fear in my dad's eyes as he locked us in the cupboard, followed by the horde of Infected that poured into our perfect little home. As soon as Joe finishes his story, the general stands and paces beside him.

"Thank you for your honesty, Lieutenant. As emotional as this story is, when you enlisted in the military, you swore an oath to serve your duty until the end. This oath is a legally binding contract, and you knowingly broke that contract and risked the lives of your entire squadron in the process."

The general pauses and continues to glare. "The fact that your squadron survived in this incident without you is irrelevant. If you had followed procedure and brought the children back to camp, we could have protected them and arranged for the appropriate level of care."

Joe's eyes harden as he quickly interjects, "We both know what the 'appropriate level of care' means, Sinter... They would have been shipped off to some badly organised refugee camp with no family, no protection and then inevitably succumbed to infection anyway. I defy anyone in this goddamned room that wouldn't have done exactly what I did! You've all heard the rumours of what happens to orphaned kids in these camps… Let's put it this way, getting infected ain't the worst thing that happens. So, if you can look me in the eye right now and tell me that you would have sent your own niece and nephew off to one of those places, then you're an even bigger monster than the Infected."

The general bares his teeth with disgust. "Once upon a time, Lieutenant, there were men and women in your squadron that may have considered you to be family too… and from my understanding, most of them have subsequently died since you abandoned them over ten years ago!"

Joe lowers his gaze slightly. "I made a choice to save two innocent children that day, and the fact that I had to abandon my brothers and sisters in the squad still haunts me every goddamn day… but the fact is, Sinter, I wouldn't even hesitate to do it all over again in a heartbeat."

Anger flashes across the general's face as his eyes darken even more. Turning to the senior officers in the front two rows of the chapel, he says, "Given the information that has come to light, I think it is unnecessary to call upon Lieutenant Suzanne Morgan as a witness. I now open the proceedings to any further questioning before we deliberate the inevitable outcome of this trial."

A few officers shift their weight uncomfortably as the general glares at each and every one of them. A female officer opens her mouth to question Joe but then thinks better of it following an intimidating stare from Sinter. It's clear from the atmosphere in the chapel that Joe has hit a raw nerve with some of the men and women in the room. Joe has never mentioned the refugee camps to us before, but I suppose from his perspective there was never any doubt that

Tommy and I would have ever reached one of those places. Seemingly satisfied that no one has any further questions for him, the general turns to face Joe once more.

"I am sure that you are aware that the punishment for desertion is death by firing squad. Do you have anything further to add before we vote?"

Joe responds with a deadpan expression. "Just vote and get it done."

The nostrils of the general's angular hook nose flare with rage. "Those that believe this man is not guilty, please raise your hand."

The silence is deafening as every single senior soldier in the entire chapel keeps their hands firmly planted in their laps. A part of me wonders if these people genuinely feel that Joe is guilty or if they fear the consequences of challenging the general. Wood creaks beside me as I quickly realise that Tommy's hands are clamped on the edge of his seat like a vice. My eyes widen with fear as I quickly whisper soothing words into his ear. The general nods his head with approval.

"Those that believe this man to be guilty, please raise your hand."

As expected, each and every one of them slowly and reluctantly raises their hand in the air. A smirk quivers at the side of the general's mouth.

"Lieutenant Joseph Hudson, I hereby find you guilty of deserting your position in the 52nd Infantry Division of Alhena, and the punishment for your crime is death by firing squad. You will meet your sentence today at 1800 hours. Please take this man back down to the cells."

Tommy's eyes begin to dilate as he jumps to his feet. A single tear streaks down his face as he clenches his fists tightly. Will wraps his arm defensively around Tommy's shoulder, making sure that he doesn't make any sudden movements.

"Take it easy, buddy. Remember the bigger picture here. We knew this was going to happen. It's all part of the plan."

Tommy speaks through gritted teeth, "How can they do this to him? Sinter is a monster!"

I grab Tommy's face to gain eye contact. "They won't be doing anything to him, Tommy… I promise."

The general quickly paces down the aisle of the chapel and stops momentarily to address us. "I suggest that you leave before six this evening. We can arrange for you to be taken back home if you wish."

My pulse quickens as I open my mouth to retort, but Will beats me to the punch.

"That won't be necessary."

Staring at us with his soulless black eyes, the general replies, "Very well."

As soon as Colt pulls the heavy wooden doors open, the general straightens his stance and then marches out the doors without looking back. The soldiers at the front of the chapel guarding Joe begin to guide him down the aisle towards us. With glistening eyes, he stares at us filled with determination.

"Everything will be okay, kids."

Swallowing my fear, I try to stop my voice from breaking. "We love you, Joe!"

A sad smile spreads across his face. "I love you too."

A couple of the soldiers guarding Joe avert their eyes in shame as they begin to push him towards the exit. Before he leaves, I can't help but call out to him.

"I didn't travel through hell and high water, to only come this far."

Will furrows his brow beside me, clearly wondering what the hell I am talking about. Joe's eyes twinkle as a smile quivers at the corner of his mouth, before the soldiers escorting him guide him through the exit. Will turns around and looks at me quizzically.

"What was that about?"

Grinning at him mischievously, I say, "I just told Joe that we are coming for him."

THE GREAT ESCAPE

We all waited for thirty minutes in agitated silence before we embarked on the suicide mission to save Joe. We needed to be confident that he had returned to his cell before we paid a visit to say our 'final goodbye' to him. Colt gathered our bags and the extra guns en route to the ominous, circular door then joined us as we began to walk down the slope to the lab entrance.

With the door now in sight, I can't help but smirk at the miserable face of Private Marshal stationed directly outside. Straightening his stance, he initially seemed surprised by our presence, but as soon as he realised that Suzie was escorting us, he immediately relaxed.

"Afternoon, Lieutenant, can you please state your business?"

Suzie gestures to us. "As I am sure that you are aware, the guardian of these kids will be executed at sundown for deserting, and the general has authorised final visitation rights."

Without questioning her further, he nods his head and reaches for the rusty lever attached to the circular door. With a loud clunk, the door swings wide open, revealing the familiar cave-like entrance into the lab.

The difference in temperature instantly makes me shiver as we approach the metal door at the far end. Private Marshal quickly pulls back the caged door, and we all squeeze into the precarious death trap that is the elevator. Once safely inside, Colt leans past me and slams his fist on the large red button. Our eyes meet momentarily before the elevator suddenly lurches downwards, plunging us all into darkness. Gripping the safety rail tightly, I close my eyes, taking a moment to focus my thoughts on the task ahead. Get in, save Joe and escape through the ventilation shafts; that's all we need to do.

Will runs his hand gently down my arm and whispers in my ear, "We got this, Ally. We can do this."

I open my eyes to see Will staring down at me intensely. His green eyes glisten in the darkness as a look of determination spreads across his face. Before I can respond, the elevator stops abruptly, sending me stumbling into his arms. Shaking his head, he chuckles to himself.

"So damn clumsy."

As I smile at Will, I notice Colt shifting his weight uncomfortably. He quickly pulls back the caged door and then paces ahead into the lab without waiting for any of us. Will guides me forward and mumbles, "What's his problem?"

I know exactly what his problem is, but of course I don't mention that. Stepping through the threshold, Will pauses and stares wide-eyed, trying to absorb this otherworldly experience. The fluorescent lighting reflects off the bright white walls, which instantly makes our eyes water.

Will looks around in pure wonder and turns to me slack-jawed.

"This place is crazy!"

Nodding my head, I say, "You haven't even seen the half of it!"

Private Marshal reaches the door ahead, swipes his key card and pulls the door open for us. He points down the corridor and past the dreaded gas chamber.

"Just go straight ahead, through the double doors and follow it around to the holding cell. You don't need to go through decontamination. I'll radio ahead and let security know that you are coming."

Suzie nods her head. "Thank you for your assistance, Private."

He stands to attention and salutes Suzie before leaving us to fend for ourselves. It appears that the holding cell is almost entirely separated from the rest of the lab, which means that the corridors that lead up to it are deadly silent. Until this point, the mood within the group has been focused and tense, but now as we silently race through the abandoned corridors, adrenaline pulses through us like wildfire.

I become so focused on the task ahead that I almost flinch when Tommy reaches up and intertwines his fingers with mine. Forcing a smile, I notice that his pupils are dilated and skin pale. I hope with all my heart that we can successfully complete the rescue without Tommy freaking out in the process. They can't know the truth; otherwise everything we have done so far will be for nothing. Within minutes, we arrive at a reception area where two young male soldiers are stationed outside a solid, reinforced metal door.

"I'm Lieutenant Suzanne Morgan, and I am here to accompany Alyx, Will and Tommy for final visitation."

One of the guards steps forwards. "Lieutenant, weapons aren't allowed into the holding cell, so you will have to leave everything out here."

Nodding her head, she begins to pass her guns and ammo to Colt. "I will escort them into the holding cell, and Colt will remain stationed outside."

The guard pulls out a key card and holds it up to the scanner adjacent to the metal reinforced door. Pushing it wide open he gestures inside.

"You guys have twenty minutes."

With my heart in my throat, we enter a dimly lit room with a neon blue light glowing behind a towering glass wall. Joe is standing directly behind it with his arms folded over his chest expectantly. Smiling, his eyes twinkle at the sight of us.

"What took you so long?"

Tommy and I run towards him, placing the palms of our hands on the glass in front of him. Suzie wavers near the door and stares at him affectionately.

Smiling at her lazily, Joe speaks with a gravelly voice, "Hey, gorgeous."

Raising my eyebrow, I mumble, "Gorgeous?"

Turning around, I stare at Suzie quizzically as a smile twitches at the corner of her mouth. "Once upon a time, Joe and I used to date… but then one day, he left me high and dry to rescue some kids or something. You always had to be the hero!"

As I spin around to confront Joe, I can't help but stare at him with my mouth wide open. "You guys dated? Why did I not know this?"

Joe's laugh is like music to my ears. "Too busy saving some kids apparently?"

Suzie rolls her eyes at him. "Sounds like a convenient excuse if you ask me. How about I get you out of here and then you can think about making it up to me?"

Joe sighs heavily. "You have no idea how long I have waited for that."

Suzie rigidly walks towards the scanner on the left-hand side of the wall. With sweaty palms, she almost fumbles with the card as she shakily holds it up and murmurs, "The moment of truth…"

Seconds feel like hours as we all stand tense, waiting to see if the key card will actually work. She swipes it over the scanner once without any immediate results, then momentarily studies the card before flipping it over and trying again. Leaning forward, she examines the scanner and holds the card up longer this time, but to no avail. Clearly distraught, she nervously wipes the back of her hand across her forehead and turns to look at us.

"Something is wrong. It's not working!"

Pacing towards her, I snatch the key card from her hand and begin to swipe the card repeatedly. The light doesn't flash either green or red. It's almost as though it doesn't even recognise Lee's key card at all. Suzie leans against the wall and closes her eyes, looking pale.

Running her hands through her short blonde hair, she speaks barely above a whisper, "He must have reported that he lost his card!"

Jumping to my feet, I begin to stomp towards her as Will grabs my shoulder to hold me back.

"What do you mean he reported it?"

Tears begin to form in her eyes as she looks past me and stares at Joe.

"I'm so sorry…"

Pushing Will away from me, I take a few steps closer and scream, "How could you let this happen? I trusted you!"

Will begins to speak hurriedly in my ear, but all I can hear is the sound of my blood pumping. Suzie slides down the wall with her head in her hands.

"I don't understand. It should have worked…"

My mind whirls as I try to run through our options. This can't be it. There must be something we can do. Stomping towards the door, I begin to gesture wildly.

"Let's take out the guards now and steal their key cards!"

Will is at my side in a flash and grabs my shoulders.

"Alyx, just stop and think about what you're saying. Just breathe for a moment, and let's think about this."

Desperation seizes me as I throw my arms up in the air. "We don't have time! We have to do something! This can't be it! It can't be over!"

I spin around to confront Suzie who continues to stare at me helplessly. The sound of Joe's calm voice breaks my heart into a thousand unfixable pieces.

"Everything will be okay, kid. Just take Tommy and get to Alhena, just like we talked about."

Anger bubbles in my chest. "No, don't you give up on me too! I need you, Joe! Don't do this!"

A smile stretches across his face as he places his hand on the glass.

"Stealing the key cards won't work, sweetheart, and so far I ain't found any other way to get out of this glass box, so you need to look after your brother and get to Alhena, okay, kid?"

Tommy stands rigidly beside me and stares unblinkingly

at Joe. My hands begin to shake as a sense of loss completely overwhelms me.

Joe leans his head against the glass and continues, "I am so damn proud of you, Alyx. You are everything that I hoped you would be. You too, Tommy. I damn well thought you were going to die and here you are… against all odds."

Shaking my head, I begin to sob uncontrollably. "Please, no…"

Will stares at me glassy-eyed, clearly sharing my heartbreak. He places his hand on my shoulder and attempts to guide me away from the glass. Joe smiles at me.

"I'll always love you, kiddo. Just remember everything I taught you, and you'll be just fine. Now get out of here while it's still light outside and don't turn back. Go on, before you make an old man cry."

Will pulls me into his arms as I continue to cry, burying my face into his solid chest. He strokes my hair and edges me towards the door. Suzie begins to peel herself off the concrete floor, whereas Tommy continues to stare at the glass like an immovable statue. With his head bowed down, Tommy momentarily turns away and briefly makes eye contact with me before spinning round and erratically smashing his fist against the glass. The neon blue light instantly flashes bright red as a deafening alarm fills the entire room. Tommy charges forwards and slams his fist into it once more, making the glass ripple and crack under the pressure.

Joe stumbles backwards in horror and begins to shout at Tommy from behind the glass. Will runs forward to stop him, but he simply pushes him aside like a rag doll before continuing his assault. I turn and look at Suzie who is standing slack-jawed and staring at the glass.

"I guess we are going for Plan B then!"

She kneels down, whips out a pistol strapped to her leg and begins to fire at the toughened glass. Amongst all the commotion, Will drags me away towards the reinforced metal door just as Colt comes bursting through the threshold. The two soldiers previously on guard duty now lie face down unconscious outside in the corridor. Colt races over to me and shouts over the sounds of the blaring alarm.

"Are you okay? What happened?"

With an almighty crack, Tommy finally breaks through the wall and showers us all in tiny pieces of glass as I say, "The card didn't work, so Tommy took matters into his own hands!"

Joe paces towards us. "I guess this ain't part of the plan?"

Colt shakes his head as we brush away the glass from our hair and clothes.

"Not even close. We can't go through the vents now – the corridors will be filled with soldiers any moment now. We'll get cut off before we get anywhere near them."

Suzie quickly interjects, "What about the service elevator? That's probably our best shot. I say we head there now and just hope that it's unmanned!"

Without hesitating, we all run as fast as we can in the direction of the service elevator. The fluorescent lights lining the clinically white corridors are now flashing dark red as an automated voice bellows, *Security breach,* through the speakers over and over again. As we skid around the corner, bullets begin to whizz past our heads from behind and ricochet off the walls beside us.

Taking cover momentarily, Suzie yells at the top of her voice, "Keep going. I'll hold them off – just get to the elevator!"

Colt drags me by the hand and runs down the corridor with Will, Tommy and Joe closely behind. Sprinting around the final corner, we arrive at the service elevator without meeting any more soldiers on the way. Will hits the button on the wall with his fist as we all spin back around and stare down the corridor that we came from. With nowhere to hide, we helplessly wait for Suzie to join us.

Colt slams his hand on the button urgently once more and then pushes me behind him, acting as a shield. Passing a pistol to Joe, he nestles his M16 into the hollow of his shoulder and then quickly stares down the sight of his gun.

Minutes go by as more gunshots echo in the distance, and Suzie is still nowhere to be seen. Feeling panicked that she still hasn't arrived, I shout at Colt over the sound of the alarm.

"Where is she? She should be here by now!"

Colt maintains his focus by aiming his gun down the corridor. "She'll be here!"

More gunshots ring through the corridor as the large elevator doors finally grind open behind us. Whipping my head around, my eyes widen with fear when I realise that it's not empty. Lying in a pile on the floor is a heap of both male and female soldiers, either unconscious or dead.

A smile stretches across my face when I see the person that is standing triumphantly in the middle. Her ice-white hair cascades down the centre of her back as she looks us over curiously with her electric-blue eyes. Tilting her head to one side, her thick black whip instantly flashes neon blue as a smirk quivers at the corner of her mouth. Joe laughs heartily beside me.

"Well I'll be damned."

THE PRIZED POSSESSION

The alarm continues to ring in our ears as we all wait anxiously for Suzie to arrive. Colt momentarily looks over his shoulder and stares at Winter as a look of bewilderment spreads across his face. Placing my hand firmly on his arm, I smile at him eagerly.

"Colt, this is Winter!"

I hesitate before I make the next comment, unsure if these are my true feelings, but as I look at the pile of male and female soldiers unconscious in the elevator, I know that my sentiment is true.

"She's a friend, and by the looks of it, she's here to help."

Nodding his head, he focuses his attention back down the corridor.

"Good, we are going to need all the help we can get."

Joe becomes more and more agitated the longer that we wait for Suzie to arrive. As soon as another spray of gunshots echo in the distance, he finally relents.

"I'm going back for her!"

Colt grabs his shoulder. "No, you're not. I'll go!"

Winter watches the exchange unfold simultaneously reading their lips. Taking things into her own hands, she runs past Colt and Joe before disappearing around the corner out of sight. Colt calls out and begins to race after her.

"Hey, you don't know what you're walking into!"

Colt slows his pace and subtly stares around the corner as the sound of a thunder crack reverberates through the corridor, followed by a flash of blue light. Suzie suddenly stumbles into view with a look of confusion on her face. Running towards us, she clasps her arm tightly as blood begins to drip on the floor. Joe races down to help her back to the elevator.

"How bad is it?"

She shakes her head. "Not bad. Just a graze, I'll be fine, and who the hell is that? Is she with us?"

Winter skids around the corner and runs towards us with her ice-white hair whipping behind her. The sound of gunshots is much louder this time as bullets begin to ricochet off the walls. We all race into the elevator and scream at Winter to hurry as Colt slams his fist urgently on the button.

The soldiers appear at the end of the corridor as the doors finally begin to move. Bullets bounce off the walls just as Winter slides in through the closing doors. Now inside, Colt and Will cry out in frustration as they attempt to force the doors shut before the soldiers reach us.

Suzie aims her gun through the narrowing gap and fires a couple of rounds before the doors finally grind to a close. The elevator begins to slowly move upwards as we all sigh with relief. Fortunately for us, it seems that the service elevator is much slower than the elevator via the front entrance to the lab, so we all have a few moments to gather our thoughts. Still clasping her arm, Suzie nods her head towards Winter.

"Is anyone going to tell me who the hell this is?"

Joe grins beside her. "Suzie, this is our friend Winter, and she's here to help us. Now let me take a look at that arm."

Colt digs into one of the rucksacks and pulls out a survival pack before quickly passing it to Joe. Suzie winces in pain as she shrugs off her jacket to assess the damage. Despite her arm looking bloody and sore, it looks as though a bullet has literally grazed her arm.

Joe looks at it closely before confirming, "Yep, you got away lightly on this one. It could probably do with some stitches and a good clean, but we can do that once we get the hell out of this place."

As Joe begins to wrap bandages around her arm Colt interjects, "Speaking of getting out of this place, I think we have a few minutes before we reach the surface. Any ideas on how we get this done without getting killed?"

Suzie's grim expression speaks volumes as Joe exhales loudly. "Well, they are going to be all over us the moment we get out of this elevator. I assume the only way in or out is through the gate?"

Suzie nods her head. "That's why this place is so secure: only one way in and one way out."

Will furrows his brow before gesturing at Winter. "Well, obviously not. Otherwise, how the hell did Winter get in? I assume she didn't waltz in through the front door? Something tells me that isn't her style."

Her eyes twinkle beside me as she begins to fumble around in her satchel. She pulls out her slate and a tiny piece of chalk and begins to scribble something down. Colt looks at me quizzically, so I quickly confirm that Winter is deaf and needs her slate to communicate. Looking rather pleased with herself, Winter flips around her slate and presents it to the rest of us. We all take a step closer to decipher her spidery writing.

Raising my eyebrows, I question, "The showers? You got into this place through the showers? How is that even possible?"

Using her wrist, she quickly scrubs at the slate and starts to write again, but before she can finish, Suzie quickly interjects, "The boiler room… behind the showers is the boiler room. The water pipes are buried underground, and they must run under the walls and outside the compound?"

Winter stops scribbling and nods her head proudly, confirming Suzie's theory. As I stare at her electric-blue eyes, I can't help but smile and be completely amazed by Winter. Not only is she one of the most skilled fighters that I have ever seen, she somehow manages to slip through the net without detection by a whole compound of soldiers. It's no wonder that this girl survives with ease out in the wilderness. The Infected don't stand a chance against her.

Colt is clearly agitated and pushes on. "Okay, great. So now that we have an exit plan, we just have to get across from one side of the compound to the other without getting shot on the way…"

It's a sobering thought, but it's our only option now. Suzie attempts to maintain morale.

"I think we can do this. Just stick together, keep our heads down, and try to lose them in the shipping containers. They will be expecting us to try the front gate."

One of the soldiers begins to stir on the floor and groans in pain. Without hesitating, Colt quickly pistol whips him on the back of the head, knocking him instantly unconscious. With only moments until we reach the surface, we all take stock of our weapons and reload our guns, as well as stealing everything from the soldiers on the floor around us. Winter stuffs her slate back into her satchel as the elevator finally grinds to a halt. We all raise our weapons and ready ourselves for the army of soldiers waiting on the other side.

Until now, Tommy has been so quiet that I had almost forgotten that he was with us. His pupils have remained dilated ever since he broke Joe out of his prison cell, and his fists are still clenched into tiny balls. Taking a step towards him, I cup his cheek to gain eye contact.

"I know that you feel anxious right now and all of this is scary, but just stick with me and we'll be okay. I promise I will not let anything happen to you."

As he nods his head meekly, Winter steps over the men and women lying on the floor and takes a stance at the front of the group. Adrenaline pulses through me as the door slowly creaks wide open. Winter holds her head up high as her whip flashes neon blue. She sprints outside the safety of the elevator and races ahead without looking back. With a pistol in my right hand, I grab Tommy with the other and follow the rest of the group, running out into the open.

The compound has turned into pandemonium as swarms of soldiers descend upon the service elevator. The same ear-piercing alarm that was blaring downstairs in the lab continues to resonate over a tannoy speaker in the whole of Panama.

My heart sinks as I realise that the damn thing must be attracting hordes of Infected outside in the nearby forest, the same forest that we have to escape through. Luckily for us, many of the guards stationed on the walls around us are leaning over and shooting at the Infected now congregating on the other side, creating even more chaos amongst the military ranks.

At the sight of us, soldiers in the surrounding area immediately open fire, unleashing a storm of bullets in our direction. Clearly outnumbered, Suzie starts shouting orders over the deafening sound of gunfire and screams at Tommy and me to keep running. Gripping his hand tightly, I begin to drag Tommy towards the maze of shipping containers while using the gun in my other hand to shoot at any soldiers directly in our path.

Colt, Suzie and Joe systematically move forward to stifle the military's progress and take advantage of the disorganised chaos around them. In a world of her own, Winter races ahead and effortlessly dispatches anyone unlucky enough to stumble across her, almost as though she has done this a million times before.

Without breaking her stride, Winter enters the narrow alleyways between the containers as Tommy and I struggle to keep up with her. Bullets ping against the metal walls beside me, making us hunker down as we sprint forward.

Reloading my gun, I quickly whip my head around and check to see if any of the soldiers have managed to follow us. Thankfully Will has finally appeared and is now racing directly behind us. With Colt, Suzie and Joe now out of sight, all I can hope is that they are following us closely behind.

Ahead, Winter suddenly disappears around a corner and is immediately confronted by a small group of soldiers. Without hesitating, she runs fearlessly to face them and raises her whip, cracking it into the chest of a formidable soldier at the front of the group.

The electrical current radiating from the whip is so strong that it sends all of the soldiers flying backwards, crashing onto the ground with arms and legs flailing. Before they can recover, Winter changes direction and runs down another alley away from the unconscious men.

The closer we get to the showers, the more my heart begins to fill with hope. Maybe we can do this. Maybe we can actually survive this. To my relief, Colt, Suzie and Joe burst out of an adjacent alleyway and appear to be unharmed. Colt's eyes glisten at the sight of me, clearly sharing my sentiment. Winter begins to slow her pace to a jog and signals for us to follow her lead.

Taking the opportunity to reload our weapons, Suzie speaks hurriedly behind us. "We are approaching the training field, and the showers are on the other side. Keep your heads down and your eyes open!"

Tommy nods his head furiously as a look of fear spreads across his face. Squeezing his hand gently, I force a smile and attempt to hide my own anxiety.

"We can do this. Just stay with me, okay, buddy? Take a deep breath. It will be over soon."

Colt, Suzie and Joe squeeze past us and join Winter at the edge of the container to assess the situation. In the middle of the training field is an abandoned vehicle, probably one that Colt had previously tampered with.

Suzie points ahead. "Okay, on my count, run for the vehicle… One, two, three!"

As our group races around the corner and out into the open, a truck screeches into our path with a machine gun mounted on the back. Colt screams at us to take cover as the soldiers immediately open fire. We all dive into the safety of the alleyway and lie face down in the dirt with our hands firmly over our heads. The soldiers fully let loose on the container that is shielding us, relentlessly ripping gaping holes in the metal walls.

Will crawls towards Tommy and me, pulling us all in closely together as the soldiers continue to fire without mercy. With my eyes firmly shut, a sob escapes from my chest as I realise that there is no way out. We are stuck in this alleyway, and we are all going to die here, torn to shreds by a hail of bullets.

As the bleak reality sets in, I squeeze Tommy tightly and scream how much I love him over and over again, but my words are drowned out by the hellfire that has been set upon us. Our eyes finally meet as shards of hot metal rain down on top of us, burning our clothes and skin in the process. In the midst of the chaos, I feel Tommy suddenly stiffen in my arms. The muscles in his arms and chest turn rock solid, and his breathing becomes more and more erratic. Releasing him from my grip, my eyes widen in fear as I realise that Tommy is about to lose control.

Pushing himself off the ground, he slams his feet against the container in front of him and cries out with exertion. Will and I stare at him slack-jawed as he grits his teeth and pushes again with everything that he has. Amazingly the container inches closer to the truck. We all knew that he was strong, but this show of strength is unbelievable. Here I was thinking that Tommy was some kind of monster, but after everything that he has done for us, after everything that we have lost, I have finally realised that Tommy isn't a monster; he is a hero.

Taking Tommy's lead, Will slams his feet against the container too and shouts at everyone to follow suit. Whether we are helping Tommy to move the damn thing remains to be seen, but the show of support, and more importantly our faith in him, only spurs him on even more. The container groans and flexes as it slowly grinds through the dirt and towards the truck.

In a blur, Tommy jumps to his feet as a growl ripples from his chest. His muscles begin to visibly pop, and he appears to grow in size. Now no longer a teenage boy, Tommy has morphed into a powerful and formidable young man. Snarling with rage, he barrels into the container like a bulldozer and manages to flip the entire thing on its side, crushing the truck and all of its occupants instantly on the other side.

The gunshots have now been replaced by silence as we all stare at Tommy in complete and utter shock. The air around him shimmers and vibrates as he continues to breathe erratically. I shakily take a step forwards and tentatively reach out to comfort him, but before I make contact he whips his head around and stares at me with black eyes. His pupils have become so dilated now that his eyes are almost entirely black, and the veins in his arms have rather worryingly darkened too. As I open my mouth to speak, Winter suddenly points at a man in the distance who is staring at us closely; he has clearly witnessed the entire scene unfolding.

From the moment I set eyes on him, my heart pounds in my chest, and my vision becomes blurry. With an expression of sheer determination, the general folds his arms across his immaculate military uniform, and he narrows his focus directly on Tommy like a prized possession. His eyes glisten hungrily and his expression darkens with a sinister edge. It's in this moment that I realise that even if we manage to escape this hellhole, the general will stop at nothing until he has Tommy in his wretched grasp.

MAN DOWN

The general sniggers as he quickly picks up a radio and begins to speak into it urgently. Feeling as if I have had the air sucked out of my lungs, nausea hits me like a tidal wave as the gravity of our situation sinks into the pit of my stomach. Now that the general has witnessed Tommy's full potential, even if we manage to escape this place unscathed, from the look in his eyes, he will send all his men and women to capture Tommy and bring him down into the lab. After everything that we have suffered, after all the pain, I'll die before I let that scumbag anywhere near my brother. As rage begins to simmer deep inside my core, the sound of Suzie's voice captures my attention.

"Okay, now that we have an audience, I suggest that we go the long way round and skirt around the training field. It will take longer, but we can't risk anyone witnessing us entering the boiler room. If we're lucky, most of the soldiers are still waiting at the gate, and if we haul ass, we should reach the showers before they get here."

The mood in the group is tense as Tommy's erratic breathing finally begins to slow down. The veins in his neck and arms are visibly darker, which is worryingly reminiscent of the Infected.

Winter takes the lead by turning on her heel and running through the shipping containers in the direction of the shower block. Will and I momentarily exchange concerned looks before he races off behind her, quickly followed by Colt.

Joe gives me a pained expression and gestures for Tommy and me to run ahead. Even after everything that has happened, I put all my concerns to one side and grab Tommy's hand.

The compound is still in chaos as the alarm continues to blare overhead. The sound of gunshots can be heard popping in the distance as the sun begins to set behind the trees. As we speedily race through the maze of shipping containers, skidding around corners and running so fast that the muscles burn in our legs, it seems that Suzie was correct in her assumption. Somehow, we successfully reach the shower block without meeting any other soldiers on the way.

Joe and Suzie are the last to enter the boiler room and slam the door shut behind them, plunging the room into darkness. Winter suddenly appears at the far side and hits the light switch with her fist, turning on a single flickering light bulb hanging precariously in the centre of the room. Six large water tanks line the walls with leaky pipes flowing in all directions. The combination of the warm temperature and the moist environment gives the room a distinctly mouldy, dank smell.

Wrinkling his nose beside me, Will mumbles under his breath, "I can see why Winter chose this place as her access point. From the state of this room, I'm guessing not many people ever come in here."

Winter races over to the centre of the room and tugs

at an ancient wooden hatch nestled in the floor. On closer inspection, it seems that this must be the service access to the water pipes underground. She swiftly sits on the edge of the hole, dangles her legs down and silently slips off the side, disappearing into the pitch-black hole below. Colt quickly rummages around in one of the rucksacks, pulls out an emergency torch and drops it straight into the ominous black hole.

Turning around to face me, he swiftly holds his hand out.

"Ally, you're up."

My mouth becomes dry as I copy Winter and hang my legs off the edge. I briefly look down and see her at the bottom, staring up at me. Her facial features are highlighted by the warm glow of the torch as a smirk quivers at the corner of her mouth. After everything that has happened here, both good and bad, I have never been so relieved to leave anywhere in my entire life.

Slipping off the ledge, I freefall through the hole, landing heavily next to Winter. Bending down, she smiles at me before holding her hand out to help me to my feet. Will leans over the edge to check that I'm okay before throwing down the bags and guns. Tommy is the next one down the hole, and without even sitting on the edge, he jumps feet first and lands with ease. Ever since the moment he lost control, he seems to have not only physically changed but mentally too. The awkward teenage boy is nowhere to be seen. He now exudes confidence, and above all, the sense of fearlessness that I often see in Winter.

Joe and Suzie are the last down the hole and bizarrely, Suzie appears to be helping Joe jump down. Groaning in pain, he lands heavily with gritted teeth. Running to his aid, I lean over to help him to his feet.

"Are you okay? Are you hurt?"

Standing up slowly, he quickly brushes me off. "I'm fine, kid. Just getting too old for all this. Don't you worry about me."

Suzie finally hangs her legs off the side, pulls the hatch shut and jumps down with a thump. Without further delay, we all scrabble around picking up the bags and weapons before following Winter through a claustrophobic service tunnel. A large, leaky water pipe runs dominantly through the centre, making the ground underneath ankle deep in sludgy mud. Suzie digs out another torch, but the dim glow provides little assistance in the pitch-black tunnel ahead.

Winter hunches forwards as the uneven ceiling slopes down even further, whereas Colt and Will, who are much taller than most of us, have to crawl on their hands and knees. Water drips from the ceiling at intervals as the roots of plants hang precariously over our heads.

In the distance, Winter stops abruptly and then seemingly points at the wall. As I wade towards her, I realise that she's not actually pointing to the wall but a crawl-hole that I assume runs up to the surface. Furrowing my brow, I can't help but wonder if an animal made this tunnel or if Winter did.

Shoving her satchel behind her, she pulls herself up and then crawls on her hands and knees, disappearing into the tiny hole. Colt shifts his weight uneasily and takes a closer look at the size of it.

"This is going to be fun…"

Becoming anxious Suzie quickly interjects, "Come on.

Let's get moving. We still have a lot of ground to cover once we get out of here."

Taking her lead, I sling my rucksack into the hole ahead of me and begin to crawl forwards. I've never considered myself to be claustrophobic, but as I stare at the burrow ahead, images flash in the forefront of my mind of the tunnel suddenly collapsing on top of us and crushing me underneath.

As I steadily crawl in the stifling darkness, dirt and rubble sprinkle on the top of my head. Trying to maintain composure, I focus on my breathing when I thankfully see a glimmer of sunlight up ahead. The exit appears to be obscured by something, probably Winter attempting to hide the tunnel entrance on the surface. A welcome rush of fresh air blows on my face as I tentatively pull back a thick curtain of ivy and vines. As soon as I pop my head outside, I look up at the wall and see that the entire thing is covered in plants and wild flowers.

Feeling a little breathless, I stare at the beauty of the lush green forest outside the compound. The plants must be attracted by the steam from the shower blocks, as they creep along the full height of the bricks. Amazingly they have even intertwined on the barbed wire at the top.

Winter stands to one side with her back to the wall. She swiftly bends down and presents her hand, offering to help me to my feet.

As I quickly scan the rest of my surroundings, my heart sinks when I realise that we have to run least a hundred metres out in the open before we reach the safety of the treeline. Winter nods her head beside me, almost as though she is reading my thoughts.

The alarm continues to blare over the loudspeakers, and the sun is finally dipping behind the trees. At least when we attempt the run we will soon have the cover of darkness on our side. Winter points down the length of the compound where a crowd of Infected have gathered on the far side near the gate.

Tommy is the next one to crawl out of the hole, quickly followed by Will and Colt. From the state of their clothes, it seems that they have all had to drag themselves on their stomachs the entire way. A few moments pass until Joe finally appears from the hole, and lastly a very anxious-looking Suzie.

As soon as she's on her feet, she suddenly launches into action. "Most of the soldiers will still be preoccupied, and even though the general saw us, I think we can safely assume that no one else knows about Winter's access. They will all be searching for us inside Panama right now, so they won't be actively watching outside the walls... but that doesn't mean that we can be complacent. After all, the Infected are not helping our cause right now.

"So, we need to split into two groups: first group will be Winter, Colt, Alyx and Tommy, and the second will be myself, Joe and Will. On my count, you guys run for the trees. Once safely across, you check the walls for any soldiers and then signal for the rest of us to run across. Got it?"

No one questions Suzie, and everyone simply agrees with her approach. As we all wait for her signal, Colt stands protectively beside me and stares at me with his steely grey eyes. Turning my focus on the tree line ahead, I attempt to steady my breathing and pull the straps tighter on my rucksack.

"On my count… One, two, three!"

We all run as fast as our legs can carry us across the open expanse. My heart feels as though it's going to burst out of my chest as Tommy begins to break away from the group. With the tree line only metres away now, we all practically dive head first and stumble into the thick underbrush surrounding the trees.

Skidding to a halt, I lean over and place my hands on my knees to catch my breath. Sweat begins to form on my brow as the familiar smell of the Infected drifts by in the wind.

Winter and Tommy are the first to react and race off into the forest, heading straight into the incoming crowd. I hesitate at first, not wanting to leave the others, but the fast-approaching Infected quickly make that decision for me. Cursing out loud, I initially fumble for my pistol but then instantly think better of it. The last thing we need is to draw attention to the sound of gunshots outside the walls. Grabbing a small hunting knife tucked into my belt, I sneak up behind an Infected and thrust my blade into the base of its skull, killing it before it even realises what's happening.

Tommy grabs the first Infected in his path and rips its head clean off with his bare hands. As the chomping head flicks black congealed blood across the forest floor, bile suddenly burns in the back of my throat. It's not the sight of the decapitated head that fills me with fear – it's Tommy's cold exterior. Temporarily distracted, an Infected suddenly catches me off guard and attempts to grab at my face. Now off balance, it falls on top of me, pushing me heavily onto the ground.

The once female Infected is so rancid that most of its face has completely decomposed. Gritting my teeth, I watch it close the distance between us and desperately attempt to claw at my face. Before I can fumble for my knife, Tommy picks up the Infected and effortlessly slams it into the side of a tree, ending its dismal existence.

As I gasp for air, the wretched thing slumps down and falls lifelessly at the base of the tree. Tommy leans over and offers me a hand, but his usual boyish expression is nowhere to be seen.

Before I take his hand, I whisper, "You are still in there… aren't you?"

A flicker of pain flashes in his eyes as he subtly averts his gaze.

"I'm still here. I think."

The uncertainty in his voice makes my eyes sting with tears. What if we're too late? What if Tommy is finally starting to change? Out of the corner of my eye is the lifeless body, crumpled at the base of the tree, a stark reminder of what Tommy could still become. Colt appears next to Tommy, having dispatched the remaining crowd, and he stares at me intensely.

"Are you hurt?"

I shake my head as he quickly pulls me to my feet and cups my cheek tenderly. "Good. Let's signal to the others and get out of here."

He continues to hold my hand as we hide behind a large tree and search the length of the walls for any signs of movement. Fortunately, it quickly becomes clear that all the soldiers have gathered near the gate. Suzie, Will and Joe appear to be huddled closely together and strangely don't seem to be watching for our signal. Will begins to pull out the contents of a rucksack while Suzie continues to talk to Joe. There's something about the urgency in her body language as she talks to Joe that suddenly puts my teeth on edge.

I whisper to Colt beside me, "I don't like this. Something is wrong. Do you think we should go back?"

He shakes his head decisively. "No, absolutely not. They probably got distracted while waiting for our signal."

Minutes race by as they continue to ignore us. My hands begin to shake as I even begin to consider ignoring Colt's advice and running back to them anyway. Finally, after five minutes of watching helplessly from afar, Will looks up to us and searches for the signal. We all conduct one final check of the walls behind them before Colt signals that the route is clear.

Will and Suzie take a solid stance next to Joe and then hook their arms around the middle of his back. My eyes widen with fear as I quickly realise that they are fully supporting his weight.

With gritted teeth, the three attempt to run across, but Joe is slow to respond. I step out from behind the tree to run across and help them, but Colt quickly grabs me by the shoulder. Will and Suzie push on regardless, and Joe even manages to pick up the pace. For the final few metres, Colt sprints out to meet them and helps drag Joe across the safety of the tree line.

With my heart in my throat, tears begin to blur my vision as they attempt to prop him up against the base of the tree. All remaining colour has faded from his face, and a sheen of sweat glistens on his forehead. Feeling completely distraught, tears begin to flow down my face as Joe forces a smile. The deathly silence in the group speaks volumes as we all stare helplessly at his blood-soaked shirt.

THIS IS THE END

We had been living in Merope for just over a year when it happened; I was seven years old, and the overwhelming sense of loss following the death of my parents had slowly started to fade. Joe had slipped into the routine of fatherhood, and the grief that he felt from losing his sister only fuelled his sense of purpose in life to be the best father to Tommy and I that we could have ever hoped for.

Like many communities thriving in this new dystopian world, if you want the benefits and the security that comes with living in a walled village, then you have to earn your place. As Joe was formerly in the military, he often volunteered to be a part of the raids where teams of men and women would leave the safety of our walls in search of any meagre supplies left over from the old world.

During these times, Tommy and I would stay with Will and his mum, who was slowly but surely becoming an alcoholic after the death of Will's dad. At the time, as children, we were none the wiser, and she managed to hide it quite well from outside eyes. Will and I would use this time together to disappear into our own little world of building forts, playing endless games and essentially living in each other's pockets. Will and I took comfort in our friendship

228

and were stronger when we were together. Both of us had experienced so much tragedy in our lives from such an early age that the overwhelming pain that we both felt only brought us together.

Sometimes Joe could be gone for days, but Will and I were so happy together I almost didn't have time to notice that he was gone. That was until that one fateful day when the group returned to Merope after having only left a few hours before.

As soon as they arrived, Will and I burst through the front of the crowd gathering at the gate to witness the worst thing since the death of my parents: Joe being carried away into the doctor's office. In that moment, all the progress that I had made, all my emotional healing from my friendship with Will was decimated in an instant. It turned out that one of the juniors on the raid accidentally shot Joe in the shoulder. It was a clean wound and fortunately didn't create any permanent damage. He was lucky, very lucky. As they carried him, he smiled at me with sad eyes. He was trying desperately to hide any evidence of pain and attempting to convince me that everything was okay, that he would ultimately survive, but I was completely and utterly inconsolable.

He spent a few days in the medical centre and throughout that entire time I refused to leave his bedside. The three of us would sleep in a bed together, and eventually when the doctor discharged him, we carried this on for months. It was at this time in my life when the nightmares returned, along with the soul-destroying panic attacks. I made Joe swear that he would never leave us or go on any of the raids again, to which he of course agreed. The crippling fear I felt from the mere possibility of losing Joe after already losing my father was too much. I had already lost one father, and I wasn't prepared to lose another. I became so obsessed with the idea that he had to be with us at all times that he could barely go to the toilet without us. I guess that's what happens when the monsters kill your parents in front of your own eyes.

As I stare at Joe now, slumped at the bottom of the tree, he looks up at me with those familiar, sad eyes, clutching his side tightly and desperately attempting to hide any sign of pain in his expression. The colour in his cheeks has faded, and a sheen of sweat has formed on his brow. In that one heart-breaking look I am suddenly seven years old again.

Panic begins to crush my chest like a vice, as I quickly realise that I am in danger of passing out. I lean against the tree beside me for support, as I try to steady my own breathing. Knowing the signs, Will is beside me in a flash and wraps his arm around my back to comfort me. He begins to whisper soothing words, but I can't focus on anything that he's saying.

My vision becomes blurry, and my mind begins to race, as I desperately search for any potential options. Joe has been my rock through some of the darkest times in my life. He is my oxygen, and I don't know how to live without him. Failure isn't an option right now, and as I stare at the grim expressions of our entire group, I only become more and more anxious.

Frustration and anger finally wins as I suddenly blurt, "We have to do something! Why are we all standing here? How bad is it, and when the hell did this happen?"

Joe forces a smile through gritted teeth. "A bullet jumped up and bit me when that goddamn truck showed up… but, sweetheart, I've survived worse than this. There's still some life left in this old dog!"

Suzie shakily runs her hand through her short blonde hair and visibly swallows before she speaks.

"I had a good look at it when we came out of the tunnel, and I've managed to patch it up well. The bad news is that the bullet is still inside his gut somewhere, so he definitely needs surgery, but providing that it hasn't hit any major organs, and we haul ass, I've seen soldiers survive similar wounds before in worse situations than this."

Straightening my stance, I feel a surge of hope pulse through me. "Okay, good. How far is the next village?"

Colt rubs the back of his neck uneasily and says, "Maybe a two-hour drive? If we floor it, we could maybe do it in an hour and forty?"

Suzie nods her head as a look of determination spreads across her face.

"Okay… Colt and Winter, go get the truck and run your asses off. Alyx and Tommy, I need you sharp and focused right now. This place is swarming with Infected, and I need you two on high alert. Joe, do you think you can walk?"

Forcing a smile, he says, "May need some help getting to my feet, but I'll be fine."

He places emphasis on the word 'fine' and stares at me directly before finally looking over at Tommy. Until now, I had been so focused on Joe that I hadn't even noticed Tommy. Studying his expression, I see a flicker of pain in his eyes as he crosses his arms defensively over his chest. Only moments before, when he fought the Infected, I was convinced that Tommy had begun to lose his humanity, but this small change in his body language fills me with hope that maybe the old Tommy is still present. How long he will be able to hold onto his humanity is something to worry about later.

Colt grabs one of the rucksacks from the floor, straps it tightly to his back and checks his guns. He looks over at Winter, and she nods her head firmly before they race off into the forest without looking back. Suzie riffles around in another bag and digs out the medical kit once more. Studying it closely, she pulls something out that resembles a pen, takes the lid off with her teeth and reveals a small needle at the end.

Bending down, she injects the medicine into Joe's arm and says, "Morphine for the pain. Give it a couple of minutes, and we'll drag you to your feet. In the meantime, drink this."

She holds the water bottle tenderly to his mouth and whispers, "You always had to be the action hero, huh? Couldn't you have just kept your ass to the grass for once?"

He swallows a mouthful of water, and a smile stretches across his face. "Ah, you know me, gorgeous, always throwing myself in the middle of the action."

Rolling her eyes, she leans down and kisses him sweetly on the lips before pushing her arm around his back. Turning around to face Will, she says, "You take the other side, Will… and, Alyx, you take his hands at the front. On my count: one, two three!"

Joe grits his teeth as we help him stand. From the glazed look in his eyes, it seems that the morphine has started to work. Suzie and Will continue to support his weight as Tommy and I pick up all of the bags and sling them on our backs. With his arms draped over their shoulders, Joe begins to trudge through the forest, swaying heavily with each step that he takes. Suzie asks both Tommy and me to spread out and search the tree line for any Infected as we set off into the unknown.

Minutes feel like hours as we all walk in agitated silence, waiting for Colt and Winter to arrive with the truck. The sun has dipped beyond the trees now and has started to paint the evening sky red. Joe stumbles momentarily as his legs give way underneath him, a worrying sign that he may be getting weaker. Despite our protests that he should pause and rest, he holds his head up high and insists that we push on further.

Eventually after thirty-five minutes, the sound of a truck can be heard racing through the trees. Even though Joe looks a little pale, we've made it this far, and he's still walking. Colt weaves dangerously between the trees as the truck grinds to a halt in front of us.

Flinging the doors wide open, Winter jumps out of the passenger seat and runs around, pulling down the tailgate. Colt rolls out some blankets on the truck bed and then helps Will and Suzie carefully manoeuvre Joe inside. As soon as we are all strapped in, Colt slams his foot on the gas and races through the forest in the direction of the nearest village. Joe cries out in pain as the truck rolls around on the uneven mud tracks. I look at Joe and then stare at Suzie, feeling completely helpless.

Nodding her head, she shouts over the roar of the engine, "We can't risk slowing down. I'll grab the last of the morphine!"

She unbuckles her seatbelt, kneels beside him and quickly administers the medicine. Unable to stand it any longer, I join her on the floor and attempt to stabilise him as much as possible.

Joe rolls his head over and stares at me with bleary eyes, then croaks, "I need to speak to Will."

I look up and stare at Will, suddenly confused, wondering if the drugs are taking effect.

"Do you mean Tommy?"

Grinning at me drunkenly, he says, "No, I mean Will!"

Suzie hops back into her seat, leaving enough room for Will to kneel beside him. Bracing himself against the edge of the seat, Joe pulls him down and begins to whisper hurriedly in his ear. The sound of the truck is so loud that I can't hear anything that he is saying, but from the look of Will's body language, he is certainly tense.

After a few moments, Will sits back on his heels and stares at Joe with glassy eyes before finally making eye contact with me. Trying to maintain composure, he sets his jaw firmly and looks back at Joe before slowly nodding his head. A smile stretches across Joe's face as he presents his hand to Will and shakes it firmly with a look of respect in his eyes.

Rubbing his calloused hands over his face, Will jumps back into his seat and stares at the floor with a deeply emotional expression. A million questions burn inside of me, but before I can ask any of them, Joe begins to cough profusely and clutches his side. His lips are stained bright red as his eyes begin to roll into the back of his head.

At the sight of the blood, Tommy and I instantly drop to our knees beside him. Tears begin to streak down my face. Pulling us down tightly, Tommy and I lie next to him on the floor of the truck, nestling our heads in the hollow of his neck. Thankfully, the road ahead seems to be smoother now as the truck is no longer rolling around.

With a gravelly voice, Joe murmurs beside us, "Remember when we used to sleep like this? You were both so tiny, and you still managed to take up most of the bed…"

Feeling panicked and anxious, tears continue to stream down my face as I smile at the memory. Snuggling my head in closer, I take a deep breath before speaking: "Listen, we're going to get through this, okay. We're going to get to the village, and the doctor will stitch you up again, just like last time. So, if you think that we took up all of the bed before, you wait until we get in bed with you later!"

Joe chuckles heartily and then begins to cough once more. Wincing in pain, he smiles with blood-stained teeth.

"You always did have your mum's sense of humour. My only regret is that she never had the chance to see how amazing you are now."

Trying to keep positive, I wipe away the salty dampness from my cheeks.

"Well, we have plenty of years ahead of us where I can continue to make you laugh. You just need to hold on a little longer, okay?"

He rolls his head towards me and kisses me on the forehead and mumbles something incoherently. Looking up at Suzie, I begin to panic. She raises her hand, trying to comfort me.

"It's probably the morphine. He's had two doses in quick succession. I'll sit here and take his pulse while watching his breathing. He just needs to rest, honey. Don't worry. I know what I'm doing, okay?"

His eyes flutter shut, and his breathing slows down as he

instantly falls asleep. Anxiety gnaws in the pit of my stomach as I lean over and gently kiss him on the forehead. Snuggling in closely, I place my head in the nook of his shoulder and take comfort in the warmth of his body.

Momentarily closing my eyes, I suddenly feel completely and utterly exhausted. All of the drama of the last twenty-four hours has destroyed me both physically and emotionally. I hope the people in this village are welcoming, and above all, have a good doctor that can help Joe.

I realise that I'd fallen asleep when Joe hunches forwards and coughs blood into the blanket. His breathing has become laboured and sweat pours down his temples. Completely panic-stricken, Suzie leans forwards and shouts at Colt, "What's our ETA?"

Colt shouts back over his shoulder, "Fifteen minutes!"

The truck lurches forwards even faster as I turn around and face Joe. My heart pounds in my chest as I lift the blanket to check his wound. The bandage is completely and utterly soaked through. All remaining colour drains from my face as I look up at Suzie.

"What the hell's happened? He was doing okay!"

Before she can respond, he pulls me in closely and mumbles under his breath, "I'm so damn proud of you, kiddo… You too, Tommy. Make sure you take care of your sister."

Tommy shakes his head and begins to sob into his shoulder. The sound of his cries breaks my heart even further as he whimpers, "Please, Dad, just hold on!"

A smile slowly stretches across Joe's face, as look of contentment flashes into his eyes.

"I could get used to that… Dad."

Joe's smile falls from his face, and his shoulders subtly relax as he lets out a long, raspy breath. Panic begins to surge through me as I stare down at him and realise that all signs of life have extinguished from his eyes. Shaking his shoulders, I cry out in despair as his pupils remained fixed at the ceiling. Suzie springs to her feet and screams at Colt to stop the truck. Pushing Tommy to one side, she frantically begins CPR. Colt flings the back door open with the medical kit in his hand and slams a shot of adrenaline directly into Joe's thigh.

Everything around me slows down as memories of the three of us flash to the forefront of my mind. The look on his face when he rescued us from the cupboard. How he would stroke my hair until I fell asleep. The smell of tobacco when he smoked a cigarette out on the porch, and when all else failed, how he would kiss my cheek and tell me that everything would be okay.

Tommy stumbles out the back of the truck and collapses on his knees, sobbing uncontrollably on the floor, a final confirmation that Tommy is still human. I clutch my chest tightly and slump forwards in pain, feeling like all the oxygen has been sucked out of my lungs. This can't be happening. This must be some kind of nightmare.

As soon as I make eye contact with Will, I realise that it must be true. He stares at me helplessly with a look of despair etched into his face, and for the first time in my life, I witness tears flowing down his angular jaw. Joe wasn't only a father figure to Tommy and me; he was also like a father to Will. When Suzie's relentless attempts to revive him fail, Colt reaches down to pull her away from his lifeless body.

Screaming at him angrily, she shoves him away and bends down to continue before finally giving up and sobbing into his chest. Black spots begin to creep into my vision as the familiar sound of white noise fills my ears. My whole world comes tumbling around me as I realise that nothing will ever be the same again.

EPILOGUE: THE ROAD TO ALHENA

It's been a week since my life was torn to shreds. A part of me can't even begin to comprehend or even remotely process what happened. In my mind, it almost feels like a surreal nightmare and any moment I'll wake up to see his face again. But then I look at my fractured makeshift family surrounding me, and I can see it in their eyes, the constant reminder that Joe is dead.

As the days begin to blend together, I have come to realise that this world that we live in is cruel and unforgiving, that life itself is a fleeting moment in the passage of time, and those that we love can be taken away in an instant. Ironically, I knew this fact once. After the death of my parents, the years of suffering that followed were a daily reminder, but happiness has a habit of eroding such truths, and my life in Merope gave me a false sense of security. I hate myself for becoming so complacent. It's a dangerous mistake that I will never make again.

The lack of sleep in the last two weeks is slowly beginning to cripple me. My body physically yearns for dreamless sleep, but every time I close my eyes, I see his lifeless expression staring back at me, and then of course, when exhaustion finally wins there are the soul-destroying nightmares that follow.

The stifling fear from the prospect of losing anyone else rots in the pit of my stomach and not only keeps me awake at night but also makes me scared to close my eyes. After all, the last time that I let my guard down and fell asleep, I woke up to find one of the most important people of my life dying beside me. I can't even fathom how naïve I was when I believed that the only thing I had to fear at night was the Infected. How wrong was I?

Tommy hasn't uttered a single word since Joe died. He has become so introverted and distant that he barely seems to be functioning. As I stare at his sombre expression, I know that I am failing as a sister, but right now I simply don't have the strength to help him. Even when I think of his name, it's almost like it becomes stuck in my throat and threatens to cut off the flow of oxygen into my lungs. How can I support Tommy in the way that he desperately needs if I can't even breathe? The continuous cycle of pain, regret and relentless self-loathing at my failures only adds to my misery.

Every day I can't help but torture myself by wondering what he would say about it. Something profound like 'death is a part of life, kiddo' and then some quippy remark to ease the pain, before rolling a cigarette and stroking my hair.

I know this is true of course, but it still doesn't help to repair the gaping hole inside my chest that his death has left behind. All I can focus on is surviving each day that comes, both emotionally and physically, then hopefully one day soon I'll be strong enough for the both of us and will be able to help Tommy survive this too.

Suzie has been the glue that has managed to hold us all together. Her sense of purpose and her overwhelming desire to see the mission to completion drives her forward every day, but underneath her tough exterior, she is just as broken as the rest of us. When sleep evades me in the early hours of the morning, I often hear her crying when she thinks no one else is listening.

It's difficult to imagine how Suzie is feeling right now because I still don't fully understand the history of their relationship, but from the brief time that I saw them together, I could see glimmers of love and affection between them. Not only did he sacrifice his career in the military for us, but he potentially sacrificed the love of his life too.

Will has flanked me ever since it happened; like a faithful guardian he watches my every move, almost as though he's ready to catch me in a heartbeat. I often wonder what they discussed in the truck that day, but right now it feels far too raw to talk about. By focusing all his undivided attention directly on me, Will has managed to push us both forward each day, even when I don't have the strength to continue. Colt and Winter, on the other hand, have focused all their energies on providing for the rest of us. Every day they work closely with Suzie to gather food, water and essentially anything that is required to make sure that we are still on track to reach Alhena.

I am glaringly aware that Colt longs to be with me. I can see it when he watches from afar, but thankfully he has given us the space that I so desperately need. I know that it hurts him every time I crawl into bed with Will or Tommy at night. He probably wishes that he was the one that I was turning to in my hour of need, but right now I need to surround myself with those that truly understand my pain, and on top of that, I can't even begin to deal with any potential dramas arising from a new romantic relationship.

A part of me wants to run into his arms and lose myself in his kisses, but I know that it would only be delaying the inevitable heartache that would follow. All I can hope is that he is willing to wait for me and that I am not too broken at the end.

Shortly after Joe died, we came across a meadow filled with colourful wild flowers blowing lazily in the warm evening breeze. We waited until sunrise and buried his body on top of a hill with unmolested views of the surrounding countryside.

As the sun rose higher in the sky, it covered the landscape in an orange glow as far as the eye could see. It was one of the most breathtaking settings that I have ever seen and a fitting tribute for such an extraordinary man. From this day forward, for better or worse, whenever I see the sunrise I know that I will always think of him.

The funeral itself was brief as we were all too grief-stricken to speak, but one of the most profound moments that took us all by surprise was when Winter held out Joe's sword and presented it to me with open palms. With fierce glistening eyes, she stared at me knowingly, almost as though she could identify with the heartbreak that I was feeling. As I took it into my hands, feeling the weight of it once more, I stared at the carved leather hilt that he had painstakingly created, the tribute to his friends and family that he lost during the fight against infection. One day, when we reach Alhena, I will add to this tribute, and I can only hope that it brings the same level of comfort to me that it once brought to him.

With each day that passes, I try to focus my mind on the journey ahead and the foreboding hurdles that are laid out before us, including the search for Mia Rose. Although she has never met her, Suzie has contacts who may be able to point us in the right direction, which will hopefully narrow our search.

Joe never fully explained why Mia would help us or potentially provide any answers about Tommy, but given our limited options, I guess we have nothing else to lose. If we're lucky, she may even have some information on the connection between Arthur Dunlop and Panama, or more specifically Al Bayati, the doctor who examined Tommy. But first we must find her in the metropolis that is Alhena without getting caught by the general.

Now that he has witnessed his full potential, I know that he will stop at nothing to capture Tommy and bring him back to Panama. Suzie confirmed that in the eyes of the general we are all fugitives, and he will be scouring the countryside searching for us. He has friends in high places, especially in Alhena, with unlimited resources that will aid our capture. Every time I picture his wretched face, rage pulses through my veins and fills me with so much hate I feel like I may spontaneously combust. He is the reason that Joe died, and I'll be damned if he even so much as lays eyes on my brother again. I'll kill him with my bare hands if I have to before he even has the chance.

As we drive through the barren wastelands and approach Alhena, clouds of sand and dust fly past the windows. The stifling midday sun is beaming into the truck, and Tommy is lying down with his head in my lap, examining the wooden figurine that Winter carved of Joe. With tearful eyes, he twiddles it between his thumb and index finger with a mournful expression etched into his face. A lump quivers in my throat as I realise that Joe probably did the exact same thing when he was all alone in his prison cell.

I have no idea what the future will bring for us. Will we succeed in finding Mia, and will she even have the answer? Is Tommy the cure for infection? Or will he end up killing us all? I guess only time will tell.

ACKNOWLEDGMENTS

Writing this book has been a real labour of love (and sometimes hate!) but I finally made it through to completion. If you're reading this and have just finished Kill or Cure, thank you so much for your time and support. I hope you have enjoyed the story of Alyx and her makeshift family. There were so many people that were fundamental in making this dream come true, so I wanted to take a moment to thank all of the amazing people that have helped to bring my story to life.

Firstly, I would like to thank two of my closest friends Rik and Magda. It's because of you I had the courage to finally complete my story and share it on Wattpad. After that one drunken night at Christmas, in a dingy old man pub in leigh-on-sea; you both told me to do what I love… and after I recovered from the terrible hangover that followed, I posted the first chapter of Kill or Cure online. So to Rik and Magda, thank you for your wise words and for all the delicious frosty beers – I definitely owe you a drink or two!

Next on the list is my family, who are a constant source of creative inspiration for me. I'd like to thank my Mum & Dad for all the years of love, support and encouragement. I'd also like to thank my brother and sister; Matt & Laura, their partners Philip & Frances, as well as my niece Ivy and the real life Tommy! Then there's my amazing new family; Gwen, Keith, Michelle & Carl, and my nieces Ella & Ava. Thank you for welcoming me into the 'Britton clan' with open arms – I honestly couldn't have wished for better in-laws.

I would also like to thank the team at Matador for giving me the opportunity to publish my novel with you. Thank you for all your time, patience and dedication. Then there's the team at Wattpad who featured my novel, which raised my profile and gave me the confidence I needed to pursue my career as an author….and then of course, I owe one huge thank you to my wattpad launch squad, who have championed my success from start to finish – you guys have kept me focussed and motivated, even when I didn't have the energy to keep writing. You are all, quite simply, awesome.

So, as promised, thanks to the following Wattpadders:

@HarrisFamilia
@Ally2028
@blisskitty
@FaithLoveMusic96
@ourheadsintheclouds
@LoveCherryNya
@LaurenOutOfTheBlue
@egonomical
@QuinnR_13
@SugarUnicorn16
@Swagperson4lyfe
@Batman_At_The_Disco
@abigurl2
@Lucythegr8t

@InternallyDolan
@ralwina13
@HuntDown_XD
@AnnetteKyzerProcop
@RutvikSavsaviya
@Danni_The_Baddest
@Papiyasarkar1
@AchinikaWijerathne
@cassandrarulez
@matthewabram
@_Wilted_Roses_
@AToby10
@debs614

Then lastly, but by no means least, I owe the biggest thank you to my husband, Adam; who over the years has been subjected to hours of questioning and late night editing of my manuscript. You have been my biggest supporter and without doubt, my biggest source of inspiration. Without you, none of this would have been possible.

Stay tuned for the second book in the Kill or Cure series.

Until next time…

Pix